THE ~~MUSIC~~ MURDER INDUSTRY

A Joe Ruddy Mystery

A.R. RATLIFF

Higher Ground Books & Media
Springfield, Ohio.
http://highergroundbooksandmedia.com

Printed in the United States of America 2019

THE

~~MUSIC~~

MURDER

INDUSTRY

A Joe Ruddy Mystery

A.R. RATLIFF

Chapter One
Who was that redhead?

The slight crack in the drapes allowed just enough bright sunlight to enter the room to wake Joe. When he felt something move behind him, he opened his eyes. He scanned the dim room until he found a familiar object. He had to do this sometimes so he would remember where he was. It wasn't that he drank every night, but when he did, he drank too much.

Joe was an ace detective after he had been awake for a while. He functioned better at night-too many years of police work had slowed down his daytime functions. Joe always had trouble when he first woke up. Sometimes he could not recall his own name, he had used so many over the past sixteen years. Oh, the problems of an undercover dick, thought Joe.

Speaking of undercover, the female voice that purred from somewhere in the bed was all it took to start Joe's heart to pounding. He had secretly feared that one day he would wake up and be greeted by a bride, whose name he would not know. Joe would sometimes joke about this fear, "I've never gone to bed with an ugly woman," he'd say, "But I've sure woke up with a few." Joe had heard Bobby Bare sing those words and had agreed with him.

Joe just passed it off as another nightmare. Afraid to open his eyes, he kept them tightly closed and tried to recall the last person he had talked to the night before.

"This is a helluva way to say good morning, but are we married?" Joe was blunt. As the little redhead opened pale, green eyes she said, "No, we are not married. What time is it?" Joe glanced at his Timex. "It's eleven-thirty," he said.

Red jumped from the bed as if she had been fired from a cannon, grabbing articles of clothing as she raced towards the door. She suddenly stopped, returned to the bed and kissed Joe on the cheek. Then running towards the door again, she shouted over her shoulder, "I'll see you again sometime Joe."

Joe searched his mind but could not remember where he had met the girl. He did not know her name, if they had had a good time, or anything at all about her. Who was that redhead? Joe thought. With a sigh of relief, he said, "Well, at least I'm not married."

Joe reluctantly got out of the comfortable bed and walked to the shower. After a long, hot shower he toweled, dressed quickly and left the motel room. As he entered the hallway he suddenly remembered where he had met the redhead. She was a barmaid at the Torn Dollar Saloon, a bar on the east side of Dallas. Joe had meant to ask her name but if he had, he had forgotten it. He made a mental note to get back to the Torn Dollar real soon.

After searching the motel parking lot for his '73, white over blue Charger, he gave up and called a taxi. Joe needed a shave, but he didn't have time to go by his apartment. When he crawled into the front seat of the yellow cab Joe said, "Central police headquarters and step on it, I'm late already."

The driver nodded and put about two hundred pounds on the accelerator. The tires squealed and smoke came from somewhere underneath the rear of the antique cab. The forward motion of the vehicle saved Joe the trouble of closing his door. As the door slammed with a loud crash Joe grasped his head in both hands.

It was a short trip to police headquarters. Joe paid the cabbie, then running, he made two long steps of the eight that led to the front door of the four-story brick building. Once inside there was another flight of stairs leading to the detective bureau on the second floor.

"What's up Harmon?" Joe asked the black detective.

"The captain wants to see you. He's pissed." Chuck Harmon said.

"Cover it for me Chuck, I've got other things to do right now." Joe smiled as he turned to leave the office.

Chuck Harmon's voice caused him to stop, "I think it's something about a homicide case."

"Well Chuck, would you tell Captain Miller that I'll be back in about an hour? I have to go pick up my car. I had to stop by here for my extra keys."

"Okay man, it's your ass," Harmon laughed.

Joe made the trip back downstairs to the police station parking lot, waved down the first black and white and got into the back seat. Most of the patrolmen on the force liked Joe. He always treated them with the respect they deserved.

"Hey, you guys wanna give me a lift to the Torn Dollar Saloon? I have to pick up my car."

"Sure Joe," said the young patrolman who was driving.

Outside, above the entrance to the one-story stucco building the torn, green dollar bill sign had no neon flowing through its veins. It was still too early in the day. There was only one car parked in the parking lot, a white over blue Dodge Charger. The young patrolman broke the silence when he asked, "Who did you go home with last night Joe?"

"Hell boys, I don't know." Joe grinned and waved as he slammed the door of the cruiser. While walking to his Charger Joe thought, who was that redhead?

Back at the detective bureau Captain Miller was screaming at Chuck Harmon for the tenth time, "Has Joe showed up yet?" Just as Harmon was about to answer the captain Joe walked into the room. Harmon didn't say anything, but he pointed towards the captain's office with his thumb.

Joe walked into the captain's office, poured himself a cup of coffee and sat down on the cheap vinyl couch.

"You wanted to see me Captain?"

"Where in the hell have you been Joe? We're not back in Germany in the army. I could cover for you there, but the Dallas police department is a whole different ballgame."

"What's eatin' you Captain?" Joe had seen Miller like this before.

"Chief Reynolds is on my ass. He wants to know if I have turned over any new leads on the Stoker homicide. He was the country singer who was shot down while performing on stage in a Dallas club. It was over a year ago, just after you got here Joe. I think I will assign the case to you." Miller did not look at Joe.

"Captain I've got a back log of better than fifty cases already. That includes more than one homicide!" Joe raised his voice.

"Well forget everything else right now. The chief wants you to work exclusively on the Stoker case. Don't leave any stones uncovered. And Joe, don't worry about the expense, this is the chief's orders. To put it mildly, right now there are only five things you have to do; eat, sleep, shit, pay taxes, and solve the Stoker homicide. Now lay out a plan and check in with me from time to time." Miller got up from his desk and walked around the office, still not looking at Joe.

He was a big man, well over six feet tall and weighed close to three hundred pounds. Miller was in good physical condition, thought Joe, looking down at his own paunch.

"Will I be covered if I have to leave the city Captain?"

"Yea goddammit, but if you do have to leave try to keep it in that thick head of yours that you will be like any other citizen. You will be undercover. No guns or police shields will be allowed out of the city. From now until this case is solved, I expect you to be humping your ass off." Miller always sounded angry.

Joe laughed at what he was thinking-Who was that redhead? Joe was curious.

"It's your hobby, writing and singing that red neck shit. You do still pick the guitar like you did when we were in Germany don't you?" Miller asked.

"Yea Captain, I still pick a little," Joe answered, "But I prefer to call it Country and Western if you don't mind."

"Well, anyway that should be useful to you while you're on this case. Don't forget to keep in touch." Miller waved Joe out of the office.

Joe raised his six foot, two-hundred-pound frame from the couch, walked over to the window and finished his coffee. Placing the cup on a serving tray on Miller's desk, he walked through the door, slightly slamming it behind him.

Joe stopped at the filing cabinets in the outer office. For the next few minutes he searched through the old homicide cases until at last, there it was, the Stoker report. Joe placed the folder under his arm, waved at Harmon and left for his apartment.

To put together some kind of new lead he first had to refresh his memory. The Stoker homicide had happened more than a year ago. He had heard about the case but had not actually been involved in the investigation.

When he arrived at his apartment, he studied the case over and over again. He read each statement, and each official document. The lines of each document appeared to become a blur as Joe's eyes became tired. Just as he was about to fall asleep Joe mumbled, "Who was that damned redhead?"

Chapter Two
Shots Fired at the Silver Horse Café

Homicide victim: Stoker, Stephen B., 29-year-old white male, occupation-professional country and western singer. Last seen alive on stage at the Silver Horse café, a nightclub in Dallas.

The coroner's report listed the cause of death as two fatal gunshot wounds to the head. The type of weapon had been a .38 caliber handgun. Steve had not felt a thing, Joe thought.

Now imagine this guy, singing his ass off and right in the middle of his performance some weirdo blows him away. Probably hated country music. Some people these days couldn't be satisfied with riding mechanical bulls, they had to shoot people to make the Old West atmosphere more authentic.

One thing was for sure, Joe had to locate this nut before he killed again, if he hadn't already. Joe had not requested this case but since it had been dumped on him, he would make every effort to solve it. Joe could understand Chief Reynolds' concern in wanting this case solved. It was bad publicity for the city of Dallas to have a nut on the loose.

Joe was snoring when the phone rang. Rubbing his eyes and picking up papers from the floor, Joe snatched the phone and placed it to his ear. "Hello," said Joe.

"Joe, is that you?" Asked a very sexy voice on the other end of the telephone.

"Yea, this is Joe. Who is this?"

"I'm Julie, you know, the girl you were with last night!" Joe heard sounds of country music in the background. She must be calling from the Torn Dollar, Joe thought.

"Sure Julie, I know who you are. What's going on?"

"I thought you would be coming by the bar tonight," she said.

"I am going to try to make it. I'll try to come by for at least one drink," Joe promised.

After Joe hung the phone up, he started to wake up some. He thought about the old days he had spent in Germany. Joe had been an Army MP. The now Captain Miller had been a criminal investigator. After his retirement from the army Miller had joined the Dallas police department, homicide division. A little over two years ago Miller had called Joe, who had been living in Ohio, and asked if he'd be interested in joining the Dallas PD. Miller had said it would be like old times. Joe needed no prompting. He had been packed in less than an hour and showed up in Dallas the next evening.

The Torn Dollar could not have been the most crowded bar in Dallas when Joe arrived. There was Julie behind the bar, the band who called themselves "A Piece of Texas", and one couple on the tiny dance floor. There was not another soul in the place.

Joe ordered a J.D. and coke, then, when Julie sat down across the bar from him, he asked, "Do you remember a country singer by the name of Steve Stoker?"

"Sure, I remember him. Didn't he have that big hit 'Holding You'?"

"Yea, that's the one," said Joe.

"I think it's awful when a good singer like that bites the bullet, so to speak. Did they ever find out who killed him?"

Joe thought for a second before answering. "No, but the case is still open. It's hard to get leads on an old case though." Joe immediately changed the subject, "What time does the band stop playing?"

"In about an hour," answered Julie.

Joe finished the drink he was holding then ordered one more, got up and walked towards the stage. He was scribbling

something on a bar napkin as he walked. Joe handed the napkin to the singer and sat down at a table near the stage.

After the singer finished the song, he was singing he said, "Lady and gentleman, we have a Nashville recording star here with us tonight. He's gonna get up here and sing some of Merle Haggard's old songs for you. Make welcome if you would, Joe Ruddy!"

Joe finished off his third J.D. and coke, set the glass on the table and made his way onto the stage. The singer, who seemed to be thankful for the break from the boredom, handed Joe his guitar and headed in the direction of the bar.

Joe sang 'Lonesome Fugitive' and 'Mama Tried'. He was on his way to becoming a recording star. If this is what it takes to solve the Stoker homicide, then by god I'm gonna sing my ass off, thought Joe. He had to get acquainted with Stoker's personal friends somehow.

Julie was all smiles when Joe returned to the bar a few minutes later. "I didn't know you could sing like that."

"I don't usually but tonight it's just part of my job." Joe was modest.

"Don't you ever stop being a cop Joe?" Julie asked.

Joe shrugged his shoulders and said, "Jack Danial's please."

Julie got him another drink and started running the one couple out of the club. When the band had finally left, she said,

"What'll it be, a quick drink for the road and then your place?"

Julie made him feel good. She didn't expect too much of Joe. I could learn to love a girl like this, thought Joe. That night Joe was sober, he knew he was not married, and he even knew her name. Still he'd had a good time. Julie was still in his arms when he fell asleep. Joe's dreams, which he tried to ignore, started but the phone rang too soon. Joe picked up the phone half ready to hear, "Shots fired at the Silver Horse Café."

Chapter Three
Nashville-A Link to Murder?

"Yea? Joe answered the phone, still dead tired from lack of sleep.

"Is that you Joe?" Miller asked, in his deepest voice.

"Just a minute, I'll check. Said Joe in an unsuccessful attempt to be funny. Miller did not laugh; he was all business.

"Have you started on the Stoker case yet?"

"As a matter of fact, I have. I'm on my way to becoming a recording star as of last night," Joe answered.

"Knock off the bullshit and get serious on this case. And Joe, try to lay off the booze until you've solved the murder. If you get anything to report just call me at the office or at my home. Keep me informed. I won't bother you again." Miller hung up and Joe went back to sleep.

The Dallas-Fort Worth airport was crowded as usual when Joe had the taxi drop him in front of the terminal. He checked his watch. He still had thirty minutes before his flight to Nashville was scheduled to depart. Just enough time for Jack Daniel's and me to have a serious talk, Joe thought.

Three shots of J.D. later and Joe was on the 707 jet, buckled up and waiting for the stewardess to start serving the cocktails, which was Joe's favorite part of any flight. I took about ten of the longest minutes Joe had ever spent for the aircraft to level off. Then the stewardess was there taking his order.

The flight was a short one. At the Nashville airport Joe rented a little red Toyota. Not because he was conservative but because it was the only car available. He forced himself behind the wheel and started the four cylinders. He didn't know for sure what his first step should be, but he had to start somewhere. Joe slipped the Toyota into drive and headed for the city of Nashville. He had a murder to solve.

The parking lot was crowded, two cars in every space. To an untrained observer this would have gone unnoticed, but Joe paid particular attention to parking lots. Parking lots told a story about what was going on inside a building. Take a nightclub for instance. If you just wanted to drink look for an empty parking lot, there's probably not much action on the inside. If the parking lot is full, chances are that something is going on inside. Either good entertainment or plenty of ladies hanging out there.

This is just like any other town, Joe thought, it just gets more attention. The last time Joe had been in Nashville he had been fifteen. But today he was here for a different reason. He was hoping to uncover a link to murder. What better place could he start to get connections with the country music industry?

Stoker had not been a big star when he had been killed. He was on his way up though. Every single record he had released was listed in Billboard magazine as a bullet. The last two bullets had left Stoker on his way down. It was a known fact; some legendary country personalities had given Stoker a little help on his way through the jungle of the music industry in Nashville. Joe would soon discover that one person in particular, had played the major role in making Steve Stoker a celebrity.

Joe had studied the case file of Stoker's murder intensely. The only unusual circumstance was that the murderer had apparently been a professional assassin, indicating a mob killing. And Steve Stoker did not appear to have a past-no police record, no credit record. Almost as if he had never existed. Nashville was the only probable city for Joe to begin this unwanted task of solving the Stoker homicide.

Solving any murder was not an easy task but solving a celebrity murder was a policeman's nightmare. Celebrities usually mingle with others who were constantly in view of the public. They did not desire to be involved with bad publicity. They were usually reluctant to discuss anything that may remotely cause them to be unpopular with the public.

Stoker was little more than an unknown, but he had potential. So much potential that some of his closest friends had been envious of him. His talent did not go unnoticed. So much had happened for Stoker in such a short period of time. Ordinarily one would have to work years to attain the stature he had received in a few short months. Stoker's luck had created jealousy among his so-called close friends.

There was a country voice coming from somewhere inside the Western club. The billboard outside the entrance displayed posters of a country group. Joe entered the club, dropped a twenty on the desk for an admission ticket. The doorman pushed the ticket and Joe's change across the desk at Joe, who slipped the change into his jeans without bothering to count it. Wandering into the main area of the nightclub, Joe took a seat at the table nearest the exit. After about fifteen minutes had gone by Joe decided not to wait any longer for the table service. He edged his way up to the bar. "J.D. and coke," said Joe, talking over the volume of the music, which he personally thought was too loud.

The bartender sloppily poured Jack Daniel's into a glass, allowing more whiskey to hit the bar than the glass. "Two dollars," he said. If I had a quarter for every one of these that I've bought someone would have to help me carry my bag of change to the bank, Joe thought.

"If you're gonna do me wrong, do it right," were the words to the song the singer was singing. Joe ordered two more Jack Daniel's, returned to his seat at the table, and forgot about everything but country music. He sang the lyrics to every song.

Joe had stopped at the Western club for a specific reason. He had heard somewhere that if you were and aspiring C & W singer and made it to Nashville, you eventually sang at least one song on the stage at the Western club. A lot of young singers had gotten their big break right here. Joe was hoping that someone here may remember Steve Stoker.

Back stage Joe talked with the singer, who billed himself as Denny Deal. Joe had not particularly cared for Denny's singing ability but had decided to ask him a few questions anyway. What could it hurt? Joe thought.

"Yea," Denny said, "I knew Steve. He took a singing gig away from me a couple years ago. That was back when I first came down here to Nashville from Kentucky. That's where Steve and me both grew up, not together of course," Denny paused.

The singer continued, "Well, I had this singing gig all lined up and was supposed to start a week later. Then Steve came in, sang one song, and ended up with my gig. Needless to say, I was very upset with the owner of the club, as well as Steve. After I thought about it awhile, I realized there was no reason to be mad at Steve. We talked on several occasions after that. Steve told me about some red necks that he used to run around with back in Kentucky. He told me how they had been involved in a few shady deals when they were kids. When I heard that Steve had been killed, I thought about that gang for some reason," Denny paused again for a moment, nervously glancing about the room.

"I didn't know a whole lot about Steve, but I hope I've helped you out." Denny finished.

Maybe Joe could come up with some kind of a lead from what Denny had told him. Joe shook the young singer's hand, wished him luck and thanked him for taking the time to talk. Something wasn't right, thought Joe as he left Denny's dressing room. There was something more than Denny's singing that Joe had not cared for. He couldn't put his finger on it right now, but Joe had that gut feeling. Denny had been too cooperative. Too quick to volunteer information to Joe, a total stranger. It was early in the investigation for Joe to speculate but that's what he got paid for. Could it be that Denny Deal was a link to murder?

That night in his motel room Joe started to think about the old days in Germany. There had been many hectic nights spent on the streets. As he slipped into a light sleep Joe knew he would dream tonight, but was it a dream or a sign?

Six long-haired German men were sitting at a table in the Picadilly bar. Their attention was focused on Joe's every move. Joe had come to the bar undercover, on a drug suppression operation for the U.S. Army. Other American military and German agents were outside the bar waiting to assist Joe with any arrests he may have to make.

When Joe's eyes adjusted to the dark, he saw the six men. He had felt their stares before he had seen them. Joe recognized them immediately from photos he had seen in the police intelligence files. They were local, small-time drug pushers. These six men, known as the Six, were responsible for thousands of U.S. soldiers having spent at least one night in the slammer. Hashish was their main merchandise and it seemed to be in great demand. Joe drank a couple of beers and started a conversation with two U.S. soldiers who were sitting at the bar.

"Do you know where I could score some shit?" Joe started. "I'm new here, just checked in from Frankfurt. I'd like to find enough to hold me over till I can get my own connection."

The soldiers gave Joe the third degree, not trusting him at first, then one of the soldiers looked towards the six German men. One of the six returned the gaze.

Joe walked over and asked if he could sit with them. The Germans were polite and offered him a seat. After the customary introductions and hand-shaking routine Joe began, in his hillbilly German, to attempt a drug buy. He knew he would have to start out smooth to convince the six that he was sincere. Joe said, "Ich merkta Rauschgift, oder hashish zu gekaufen, bitte." ("I would like to purchase drugs or hashish, please.").

The six suddenly became silent after the subject of drugs had entered the conversation. Joe had spoken too soon. The six would admit nothing to him now so Joe finished his beer and returned to the bar.

About ten minutes later the six men left the Picadilly. Joe thought, the possibility of scoring with the Six tonight is out of the question. After paying the bartender Joe too left the bar.

Once outside Joe hung around the front of the club. A mixture of German civilians and American GIs were leaning against the building-some even lay on the sidewalks. Real class people, most of them high on something or hoping to be high soon. Joe took a few mental pictures of the derelicts' faces and walked off to another 'head joint'.

Turning right into the dark alley, Joe had no idea what lay waiting for him there. "Get that son-of-a-bitch!" A loud voice boomed in his right ear. Joe felt a vice-like hand grab his right arm and lift him off his feet. He nearly woke up at this point in the dream. At about the same instant Joe felt a blow on the side of his head. He tried kicking but four arms held him now, eight feet were kicking him.

Almost unconscious, Joe thought he could see one very big hand tearing his shirt sleeve. When he realized what the Six had in mind it became Joe's nightmare.

"Hold this asshole," one of the men said.

"This pig's gonna try some good shit," grinned another. Hearing this Joe gave one final struggle as he saw the hypodermic syringe getting closer to his arm.

The next morning Joe woke up refreshed. He was thinking about Stoker even before he was totally awake. As he crawled from the bed, he vividly recalled the dream. Joe felt there had to be some reason for him to recall in a dream, an incident that had actually occurred more than ten years ago. As he dialed the telephone, he could not stop his hand from shaking. He knew he was on to something big. Miller answered on the sixth ring.

"Hello."

"Hey Captain, I think I have a lead. See if you can get a make on Stoker's family. They are from somewhere in the hills of Kentucky. If you get anything just call me back at this number. Are you ready to copy?"

"Sure, you know I'm always ready." Miller joked.

"The number is 737-243-5353, extension 10. If I'm out leave a message. That's all I have for you this time." Joe could feel it stronger now. There had to be a link to murder right here in Nashville, Music City, USA.

Chapter Four
Nashville, Day Two

Stoker may have been straight, but Joe had never met anyone without a past. It was a sure bet that some of Stoker's past had been spent right here in this city, Joe thought as he snaked his way through the dancers. They had just finished dancing to 'Cotton Eyed Joe' and were on their way back to their tables. Joe was trying to clear himself a path to the bar.

"What'll it be?" Asked the bartender, when Joe had finally arrived at the bar.

"I better have two J.D. and cokes," replied Joe, "It's too far to walk up here every few minutes."

While the bartender was mixing the drinks Joe asked, "What time does Denny usually show up?" The bartender gave Joe a strange glance then said, "Denny? That's his band you're listening to right now. Denny won't be here though."

Joe wasn't sure he had heard correctly; it was loud in the club. "How's that again?" Joe asked. The bartender was not the talkative type. He just stared at Joe and said, "Man, I remember you from last night. You sure ask a lot of questions. Denny quit. Said he got a contract to do some recording work. Didn't say where he was going though."

Joe had been correct, he was sure of it now, Denny knew more than he had been willing to tell. If Denny was still in Nashville, Joe had to find him. The next time Joe talked to Denny Deal he would use a different approach. He was positive that Denny had the answers to some very important questions. Day two in Nashville may turn out to be a very interesting day after all.

Joe left the Western club. In the parking lot cars were slowly cruising. Not an empty parking space could be found. If they were coming to the club to catch Denny's performance, they would be disappointed, Joe thought.

Before Joe got within ten feet of the rented Toyota, he noticed a paper had been taped to the windshield of the car.

He removed the paper, opened the car door and got inside. The dome light was bright enough to provide ample light to illuminate the note. Joe could not believe his good luck as he read it,

You ask too many questions. I don't know who you are

but if you are interested in Steve Stoker, you might

try his former girlfriend/manager, Susan. She lives

in Nashville.

Someone is trying to be helpful, Joe thought. "Sure wish they had left Susan's last name," he said aloud. Starting the Toyota, he placed the car in DRIVE and pulled out of the parking space. He had no sooner moved his car when another car pulled in. Joe was even more convinced now that Nashville was the place to stay until some very important questions were answered.

Susan was about to hear from someone named Joe. If she knew anything about Steve Stoker, Joe was going to know it too, before he left Nashville. It was his business to gather information. And he was not above a little deception if that's what was required to obtain a lead that could possibly solve a homicide.

It was early in the evening when Joe returned to his motel room, he had some phone calls to make. Thumbing through the yellow pages he found the number he was looking for. He dialed the phone, one ring… two rings…, "The Western club," was the answer.

It was a long shot but possibly the only shot Joe would have. "Is Susan there?" Joe thought, chances are Susan spends some time in the club.

"Yea, who is this?"

"Denny," Joe coughed in an attempt to disguise his voice. There was a brief silence on the line.

"She's here Denny, but I'll have to find her. Hold on." Finally, someone who identified herself as Susan answered the phone. "Yea Denny, what's the problem?" the voice inquired.

"Susan, could you come by the Music City motel, Room ten? Something terrible has happened and I think you should know about it. I can't talk now. I'll meet you at the motel in half an hour."

The line was silent again as Susan thought. "Okay Denny, I'll be there but you better have a good explanation." Susan sounded angry.

Joe removed his shoes and stretched out on the bed waiting. If Susan showed up it would be a damned good indication that she knew something. If she didn't show, then Joe would keep trying to locate her. He rubbed his eyes and tried to concentrate on the news broadcast on television. First Joe lay on the bed then he was pacing the floor. He'd always hated the waiting. Anticipation was always worse than the dangers of the streets, anytime, Joe thought.

The slightest noise had him running to the window to pull back the drapes and peer into the parking lot. After about twenty minutes Joe saw a blue, late model Cadillac, one of those with the chopped off rear-end, park beside the Toyota.

When the car door opened the inside light flooded the interior of the Cadillac. She was alone, a very attractive blond. She appeared to be in her early forties. The lady was stylishly dressed and had a very healthy appearance. This must be Susan, Joe thought.

It seemed like an eternity before the knock on the door. Joe quickly opened the door, grasped Susan's arm and pulled her into the room. When he pushed her onto a chair Susan, made an attempt to catch her purse before it fell to the floor.

"Hey goddammit, what's the idea here? You're not Denny!"

"I didn't think you'd notice," Joe said, using his 'tough guy' voice. "Look bitch, I'll be right up front with you. This puke Denny, the asshole has left town. Only thing is, he forgot to leave a forwarding address. Since he is into me for five grand, I thought you may want to help him out." Joe studied her face for some kind of sign, but there were none. This girl is as hard as nails, he thought, as she answered.

"Look, I don't know what you're talking about. Denny didn't tell me anything. That's why I came here tonight." She sounded convincing enough.

"What do you have going on with Denny?" Joe demanded.

"We are just friends," was her answer. "I wanted to find him too. I have an interest in Denny. I am his promoter and I helped him get started in the business. He has run out owing me quite a bit. I advanced him some money on his contract and just found out tonight that he is no longer playing at the Western club."

Joe detected a slight sound of displeasure in Susan's voice. "Did you help Steve get started too?" Joe tried. Still no alarm showed on Susan's face.

"In a manner of speaking, Steve and I helped each other. He wrote and sang the songs and I had the connections. Steve actually worked for me; we had a contract. I owned Steve Stoker."

I must have struck a tender spot, Joe thought. Susan was telling him all about Stoker as she continued.

"Once Steve started getting all that attention, he pushed me aside. I suppose that he didn't want to be seen with me." Susan stopped talking.

Joe thought he had better get Susan calmed down. If he could get on her good side, she may be able to help him-in more than one way. "Look, I'm sorry I was so rough on you," he apologized.

"Let's just forget about all of this. What's your game anyway? Why all of the questions about Steve all of a sudden?" Susan didn't appear to be too upset now.

"Steve owed me. I wrote some songs for him back in Kentucky. One day, when I heard one of the songs I'd written on the radio, I thought it was time for me to look Steve up. I was a little late, he's dead now." Joe lied, hoping Susan, who was no fool, would not detect the deception.

Then Susan softened some and started to talk to Joe. She told him about how she had always been attracted to younger men. It had always caused problems. She would get them started, make something of them, then lose them to a younger woman or they'd get hooked on drugs. Joe almost let himself feel sorry for Susan but, he thought, maybe this was her standard opening line.

Suddenly he thought of an off-the-wall scheme. "Who are you promoting right now?" He asked. Susan stared blankly at the floor and sighed, "No one since Denny has run out," she replied, almost in a whisper.

Joe continued, "It's been a while since I have performed but I do write songs. If you are interested, you could make something out of me. I'm almost broke and I was going to be looking for a job soon anyway."

"I'm not sure I want to get involved with any more singers right now," Susan said flatly.

"Look, you could check out some of my material and if you like it who knows how far we could go together. If you don't like it then you won't owe me a dime." Joe presented his pitch.

Susan got out of the chair where she had remained since Joe had so violently pushed her into it. She began to crawl on the floor, recovering the contents that had spilled from her purse. She had not yet responded to Joe's offer.

After she had managed to arrange her purse, she handed Joe a business card. "Call me tomorrow and make an appointment. I probably should not do this; you were such a prick tonight. Maybe it will be worth my trouble. Could I go now?" Susan pointed at the door.

Joe had not realized it, but he was still blocking her path to the door. "What? Oh, sure," Joe said. Moving from his position in front of the door. "Susan I really am sorry that we had to meet like this, but I am glad we met." Joe was apologetic.

Susan opened the door, saying, "Don't forget to call."

As soon as Susan had gone Joe started to pack. He checked out of the motel ten minutes later and was driving around Nashville looking for a place to spend the night. If Susan had any thoughts of reporting this incident to the police or having some of her friends return his hospitality, he would be hard to locate. Instinct had always paid off for Joe. He was not going to start ignoring his instinct now. After a day like day two in Nashville, Joe was ready for a cool J.D. and coke.

Chapter Five
I'll Write the Lyrics

Changing motels meant a phone call to Captain Miller. Joe had to let Miller know where to reach him in case something developed in Dallas. Joe dialed the number he knew so well by now. It took several rings before Miller answered.

"Do you know what time it is?" Miller's voice was unmistakably angry.

"Captain I just called to let you know that I had to change motels. I have a new phone number for you to reach me at. I think I have just met someone who can help me get started in the business. I'll know more tomorrow." Joe gave Miller the new phone number.

"I haven't gotten anything back on the Stoker family yet," Miller said, his tone of voice less angry now. "I'm expecting something soon though. Do you have anything else for me?"

"Nothing concrete has developed yet Captain."

"Then get off this damned pone so I can get some sleep. Some of us do have to work you know."

"Goodnight Captain," Joe said and hung up.

Joe found it hard to believe that he was actually being paid for something he enjoyed doing. He started to hum and talk to himself. "Let's see," he started, "The tools of a song-writer are paper, pen, and for sad songs, I have it-a bottle of Jack Daniel's." Joe searched through his luggage until he found all three items.

I don't want to make you cry,

So, I won't ask you why you are leaving

Joe started to write a song. He wrote another line that did not please him. He scratched through it and started the second line over;

I'll just let you go,

and if you want me to know you are leaving

So far, it's not too bad, he thought.

The next step was to get a guitar and put some music to the song. Then he would play it for someone who had an ear for determining what would be a hit.

Over the years Joe had written several songs but until now he had never seriously considered recording any of them. Most of his performances had been in bars and nightclubs, and occasionally at friend's parties. This may be his one and only chance to prove himself as a songwriter. Joe took a long swig straight from the bottle of Jack Daniel's. It was working already. He could feel another song coming on;

I only have one bottle to get me through the night
So, I'll hold this bottle while he holds you so tight
When this bottle's empty the pain won't disappear
When I wake up tomorrow, I know you won't be here

You won't be here, but it comes as no surprise
I expect anything to happen when a woman cries
We won't be together that's one thing you've made clear
This bottle holds the reason why you won't be here

I only have one bottle and I've just took the first drink
I've heard it helps me to forget when I don't want to think
Whiskey gives me courage and helps me hide my fear
But it won't bring you back to me, no you won't be here

I've only got one bottle and now it's almost gone
I should go to bed now so your mem'ry can come home
The way I've been acting made you think I don't care
But I'll always love you though I know you won't be here

It was after 11:00 A.M. when Joe woke up the next morning. He was still dressed, hugging an empty Jack Daniel's bottle. There were papers scattered all over the floor and bed. Shuffling through the papers he found at least five songs he thought was worthy of recording.

For the first time since she had given it to him, Joe removed Susan's business card from his wallet and looked at it.

Printed on the card was;

Jordon Music Industry Enterprises
Promotions, Publicity Arrangements
Call Susan Jordon-234-7896

Joe dialed the number and was greeted by a pleasant female voice, "Jordon Enterprises, may I help you?"

"Good morning. I'm Joe Ruddy, Mrs. Jordon asked me to make an appointment to see her today." Joe yawned.

"Yes Mr. Ruddy, Susan mentioned something about you. She will see you at 2:00 P.M. today."

"Thank you, I'll be there." Joe hung up the phone, showered, dressed quickly and left the motel room.

Checking the address on the card Joe started the Toyota and pulled the car into the traffic. He stopped at the first Exxon station for gas and directions to Magnolia Street. The gas station attendant told him he was only ten minutes away from Susan's office.

After driving a few blocks, he turned left onto Magnolia street. Joe slowed the vehicle to check the numbers of the expensive homes. At last he found it. Magnolia street, number 612, was a two-story, brick house. It had been designed after an early French construction. Joe parked the Toyota, got out of the car and walked to the front door. He rang the doorbell and waited.

The oversized door opened, and Joe feasted his eyes on the most beautiful brunette he had ever seen. She was just over five feet tall and had a great tan. She can't be more than twenty-five, Joe thought.

The brunette was dressed casually in gray pants and a blue sweater. Joe noticed that she wore slightly too much makeup to suit him. Although she was not glamorous, she was certainly easy on the eyes.

"You must be Joe," she spoke. "I'm Carla. Come in, I have been expecting you." After he had entered the house Carla motioned for him to be seated on a sofa, just inside the door. "Susan will be with you in a moment. Would you care for something to drink while you wait?"

"No, I'll just watch you if you don't mind," Joe said jokingly.

Carla blushed and sat down at a small desk, just across from the sofa, and started typing. Joe had a perfect view of Carla's covered legs underneath the desk. Too bad she had them covered, he thought. I have a feeling she is hiding legs worth seeing.

Joe's sensuous thoughts of Carla were pleasantly interrupted by Susan's entrance into the room. She was dressed in blue jeans and a tee shirt and appeared much younger and more vibrant than she had last night.

At first Susan offered Joe her hand, then, as he stood, she pulled her hand back quickly and said, "After last night I'm not sure I should trust you. Did you bring any of your material with you?"

"Yea, I wrote several songs last night but have decided on five of them to play for you. Do you have a guitar?" Joe asked.

Susan turned to Carla and said, "Carla, get the man a guitar."

As Carla got up from the desk Joe's eyes followed her movements. Susan did not fail to notice this. When Carla was out of the room Susan spoke. "Don't get any ideas about Carla. She is here for one thing and one thing only. She is my private secretary and she's a damned good one. Let's keep it that way." She let Joe know exactly how she felt.

"I wouldn't have it any other way," Joe smiled.

Carla came back into the room carrying a Martin guitar in its case. "I don't know if it's tuned but this is the best I can do for now," she said apologetically.

Joe accepted the guitar, removed it from the case and checked it for the proper tuning. A good Martin guitar keeps its tune for a long time, he thought.

In a few minutes Joe had the Martin tuned. He started to sing one of the songs he had written the previous night.

"Here I am wishing you were here. It's a dream that won't come true I fear."

Joe picked the guitar and sang as if he were performing for an audience at the Grand Ole Opry. When he had finished, Susan and Carla applauded.

"Now that's what I call country music! Where have you been hiding Joe?" Susan asked.

"Does that mean you think I've got a chance?" Joe sounded surprised.

"Sure, you have more than a chance. There's a whole world full of people out there, Joe. Believe me, a lot of them like to hear your kind of tear-jerkers. Will you write the music too?"

"No, I'll write the lyrics. I can't read or write a lick of music," Joe said truthfully.

"Well, that doesn't matter right now. We can work with what you do have then later we can do the fine tuning. Boy, you are going to be a country star, and damned soon," Susan assured him.

Carla was standing close behind Susan and Joe thought he saw her wink at him.

"Get him set up Carla," said Susan. "Write him an advance check and help him out. And Joe, be here tomorrow at 9:00 A.M. and be ready to sing. I'll have some people here who are big in the music industry. I want you to have a chance to do some rehearsing with a band before they get here."

Susan offered Joe her hand again. This time she did not pull it away as he took the smooth hand and gently squeezed it. She then walked casually out of the room.

Carla was smiling as she returned to the small typing desk. She sat down and wrote Joe a check and handed it to him. She said, "This is only an advance of 500 dollars. It should take care of you for a few days. Susan likes to keep in touch with her people, so I'll write my home phone number down for you. If you should have any trouble, please contact me here at the office or at my home. I will also need your phone number and all that..."

Joe accepted the check and thanked Carl then returned to his motel room. As he entered the room, he noticed the red light on the telephone was flashing. There was a message for him at the front office. Joe dialed "0". The motel operator answered. She gave Joe the message to call Dallas. The number was Captain Miller's office number.

Joe dialed the Dallas number and Captain Miller's voice boomed on the line. "Hey Joe, I got a make on Stoker's family. Stoker was an alias. He was born Stephen Cranston. His father is James Cranston of Richmond, Kentucky. I attempted to contact the PD there but it's a small town, I never could contact anyone. I talked with the state police and they said that Cranston lives on route one. I don't think you'll have any trouble finding the place." Miller sounded excited.

Joe related to his captain all about his break in the music industry. With all the news out of the way the conversation ended. With a quick goodbye, both men hung up.

At 9:00 A.M. sharp Joe was ringing the doorbell at 612 Magnolia. Susan opened the door. She had not bothered to dress yet and still wore her house robe. Even this early in the morning she was attractive, Joe thought.

"Good morning Joe. Come on in, I'll get dressed and be with you in a couple of minutes. Is it nine already?"

"It sure is," Joe said, checking his Timex.

"The recording studio is the third door on the left, that way." Susan pointed down a long hallway. "Go ahead and look around if you'd like." She left the room.

Joe stood alone in the middle of the room for a few minutes then decided to check the studio. When he opened the door, he was surprised to find a fully equipped recording studio. "God damned, there must be a hundred grand tied up in this room," he said.

There was a recording booth with at least twenty microphones arranged in various positions. Hell, a whole orchestra could perform here, he thought. There were mixing boards and sound effect machines. Equipment Joe had not known existed, not to mention its function. As he admired the equipment he became totally involved and did not hear Susan enter the room.

"Joe did you write anything new for us?" She asked.

"No, I thought I would do some of my earlier material this morning. Where is the band?" Joe asked, impatiently.

"They will be arriving any minute."

Joe sat down in a large leather chair by one of the mixing boards. "Do you operate any of this equipment?" He asked.

"No, my husband was the sound expert, before he died a few years ago. I have just kept the studio up to date with the latest in technology. When we do recording sessions, I hire a sound man to come in and take care of the technical operations." Susan did not volunteer any further information concerning her dead husband and Joe did not want to raise her suspicions by asking too many questions. There would be time later to pry.

About fifteen minutes later the first members of the band began to arrive. Within thirty minutes all the musicians were there. They did not have to bring any of their own equipment, so they were ready to start rehearsing immediately. One older gentleman, introduced to Joe as Bob Simms, said, "Okay Joe, this is the part where you take the old box and hack out one of them tunes you wrote. We'll pick up on it and take care of getting the music right. When we get it worked up then Sam over there," he pointed, "will set it to sheet music."

Joe picked up the Martin that Carla had given him the day before. He started to strum then sang,

"Something strong, like Jack Daniel's straight.

And could you hurry, I'm already late..."

About an hour later the band had worked up three songs. Then Bob Simms asked, "Joe, do you want to play rhythm on these songs or are you just going to sing?"

Joe had relaxed around the musicians now, as he answered, "You guys play the music, I'll try to sing, and I'll write the lyrics."

Susan sat through most of the rehearsal then she left the room. She returned about ten minutes later, she looked worried but continued to smile. Joe noticed this and was curious.

Bob Simms felt that the songs had been practiced enough and he told everyone so. "We are ready to record them," he told another band member named Zack. Zack was the audio technician for the band. A few minutes later Zack had the recorder ready and the session started. By noon there had been six songs taped. The mixing would be done later.

Later that morning the band had gone, and Susan was playing the tape for the third time. Finally, she spoke. "Joe, I think we have something here. Now if we can just convince the gentlemen who are coming here today. I know them very well. They all have good ears for talent. Each of them has been very helpful to my career in the industry."

Joe ate a quick lunch with Carla and Susan as he anxiously awaited the afternoon. At 2:00 P.M. the first one arrived, the other two immediately after. Susan introduced Joe to each of the gentlemen. There were Robert Wesley of MTM records; Paul Thompson of Stir Publishing company; and Gregory Stoner, Program director and disc jockey of WQCA radio station.

Susan led the way into the recording studio. She asked everyone to be seated then she began. "Gentlemen, I have discovered a singer. His name is Joe Ruddy, and I think he is just what the public is ready for. I appreciate your coming by to listen to this new talent. Shall we begin?" Susan walked over to the recorder control panel, flipped the toggle switch that started the tape player, then sat silently in the leather chair.

These three men had listened to thousands of would be singers. Just having them agree to listen to your song was an accomplishment and an honor. Joe tried to make some determination of what their opinions were by observing their expressionless faces, it was impossible. All three men sat there, not revealing any emotion. After the tape had played, Mr. Wesley asked Susan to run it again. Joe excused himself and nearly ran from the room.

Carla was at the typing desk earnestly typing. She did not seem to notice as Joe sat down on the sofa across from her. "Thought I would come out and chat with you. I can't stand the suspense in the studio. Do you mind?"

"No, I don't mind," Carla answered nervously, not raising her eyes from the typewriter. She seemed reluctant to talk for some mysterious reason. She occasionally looked down the hallway at the recording studio.

She must have read my thoughts yesterday, thought Joe, as he admired Carla's beauty. Today she was wearing a very unstylish, short yellow skirt. As he sat across from her now, she noticed him staring under the desk. She was aware of the effect she was having on him every time she crossed her tanned legs. She didn't seem to mind Joe sneaking a peek, so he continued to gaze overtly.

"How about dinner tonight?" He invited.

Carla glanced down the hallway again. "Sure Joe, call me about six. You have my number."

Joe couldn't help but notice that Carla seemed upset. "I'll leave you to your work then," he said, taking one more obvious glance at her legs.

Before Joe could make it back into the studio the meeting had terminated. Everyone was standing, saying their goodbyes. Mr. Wesley kissed Susan on the cheek and Joe noticed that Wesley was prolonging his departure. Susan asked Carla to show the gentlemen out. Then she turned to Joe and said, "Well, that's over with, phase one. We should know something within a week. These guys are prompt and if you have talent they will be interested. Next week we may be talking contracts."

That evening Joe arrived at Carla's house at 7:00 P.M. She had made reservations at the Golden Pheasant, a nice restaurant in east Nashville. During dinner Joe tried to keep the conversation directed towards Susan. He desperately required information concerning Carla's boss for his investigation. Carla was quiet and very protective of Susan and carefully chose her words. Joe felt that this loyalty and silence act of Carla's went deeper than an employer-employee relationship.

After dinner Carla invited Joe, not to just have a drink at her place, she was much too liberated for that. She asked him, "Would you like to spend the night with me?" Joe leaned across the seat of the Toyota and kissed her on the cheek. "Babe you're playing my tune and I'll write the lyrics later. Right now, I have some unfinished business that must be taken care of, tonight. But hold the invitation until later this week."

Chapter Six
Stoker's Past

Interstate 75 north was not crowded at that time of the evening. Joe had called Carla and explained that he would be out of town for a day or two. He had not decided to go to Richmond until he had returned to his motel room from dropping Carla at her place.

"If Susan is looking for me make an excuse," he had said to Carla. Then he packed a change of clothes and was on his way to Richmond. Joe had not given the murder much thought for the last two days. He would have to be in the right frame of mind for the visit to Stoker's hometown.

Driving had always made him hungry but tonight he was trying to resist the urge to pull off the interstate. Joe knew that if he did stop, he would be impelled to fill up on junk food. He did not need to gain any more weight. "I tried jogging, but it always took so long to get to where I was going. I had to give it up. I was always late."

At 3:00 A.M. it was sleep, or lack of it, that forced Joe to stop at the Holiday Inn. He was only twenty miles from Richmond. I'll sleep for a few hours then I'll feel more like investigating a murder, Joe thought.

He checked into the room and finally admitted defeat. He dug in his pockets for change. The craving he had for junk food could not be denied any longer. Joe went to the snack center in the lobby of the motel and returned to his room a few minutes later with two sodas, potato chips and cake. This should hold me until breakfast, he thought.

At 7:00 A.M. he was on the road to Richmond. By 7:30 he already had directions to James Cranston's farm. After about an hour of driving Joe found the dirt road that turned off the main highway. He signaled and made the left turn.

He followed the road for about one mile to the top of a hill. From this vantage point Joe could see a large clearing just ahead. There was an enormous white farmhouse constructed in the center of the clearing. The country scene was complete with a typical red barn, located behind the house. As he approached the farmhouse Joe noticed another hill to the right of the main structure. Here he noticed several house trailers, and vehicles of various make and age were parked near the barn. Some of the vehicles were in bad shape, dented and rusted.

As he pulled into the driveway a pack of dogs ran towards the Toyota. He was not getting out of the car. Inside he would be relatively safe, outside he would be dogfood. The dogs looked mean enough to tear Joe to shreds.

An older man with balding, gray hair, dressed in faded blue overalls stepped out of the house and onto the porch. He shouted something that Joe could not understand. The dogs stopped their barking and all, but one ran back towards the rear of the house.

Joe remained seated and rolled the car window down, prepared to roll it back up if it became necessary. He spoke to the man.

"Sir, I'm looking for James Cranston."

"That's me, what can I do for you?" Asked the old timer.

"I would like to talk to you about your son, Steve." Joe replied.

Cranston walked out to the car, bent over and took the dog's collar in his right hand, "Now old king here might bite a feller, if he don't know you. I'll hold him while you walk on up to the house."

Joe was thankful that the old man was holding the crazed animal. As soon as he was safely on the front porch, Cranston freed King then offered Joe his hand.

"What is it you want to know about Steve?"

"When was the last time he was home?" Joe had to start somewhere.

"Let's see," the old man scratched his chin. "I think it was two years ago. That was the last time we ever saw the boy, alive. Steve was twenty when he left here. When he came back two years ago, he was happier than we had seen him for a long time. Some of his friends came over to the house and they had one helluva a party. Steve was just getting started in the music business then."

It was apparent that Cranston had cared for his son and was still very proud of Steve. Joe listened respectfully for a few moments before he continued.

"Was there anyone with Steve when he came home two years ago?" Joe tried a new approach.

"Yea, he had some little dark-haired girl with him. I think her name was Carol or something like that. We can ask Steve's mother. She's in the house."

Joe trailed Cranston into the house and into the kitchen, Mrs. Cranston, a sweet little, gray haired lady was sitting at the table. After she had been introduced to Joe, she offered him coffee.

"Thanks, black please," Joe accepted.

Mrs. Cranston was not as talkative as her husband. She told Joe that the girl who had been with Steve was named Carla.

"They told us they was thinking about getting married. She was a pretty little girl, and just as nice as she could be."

Then Joe asked if they knew anyone that would have a reason to kill Steve. Mr. Cranston replied, "Lord no, Steve was an easy-going boy. He was well liked. We never knew of him hurting anyone." Joe had expected a similar answer from a parent.

Mrs. Cranston started to cry. Her husband tried to comfort her. Joe had heard enough and did not want to further upset Steve's mother. After he had gotten some names and addresses of Steve's friends Joe thanked the Cranston's and started to step off the porch. King had other ideas. Joe pulled his foot back onto the porch in one swift movement. Cranston restrained King again, allowing Joe to safely return to the Toyota. Joe waved and the Cranston's returned the wave. What a relief to get away from that pack of wild dogs, he thought.

After a few more stops in Richmond Joe discovered that most of Steve's former friends no longer lived in Richmond. They had left this small town to find work elsewhere. The few Joe did talk with could not add anything the Cranston's had not already told him. He had just one more address remaining then he would return to Nashville.

It was already getting dark as Joe stopped in front of the gray, one-story, wooden frame house. He expected a quick interview with Gary Turner, the former best friend of Steve Cranston.

As he approached the house Joe did not think anyone was home. There was a dim light from somewhere inside the house, but it was barely visible from the outside. Lightly rapping on the door, Joe shifted his weight from his left to right foot as he waited impatiently. A few seconds passed then a young man opened the door. He was about Joe's age, maybe a little younger, Joe guessed. He wore his hair very long, a style that had been popular in the late sixties. The man was wearing blue jeans and an army fatigue shirt. The sleeves had been cut away from the shirt.

"What can I do for you?" asked the man.

"I'm looking for Gary Turner," Joe answered.

"I'm Gary." The man said bluntly.

"Do you mind if I ask you some questions about Steve Cranston?" Joe hoped he could hurry with this interview. He felt uncomfortable around this man.

"You a cop?" Gary asked.

"No, I'm an insurance adjuster. There are some things that have to be cleared up before my company can settle Steve's claim," Joe lied. He felt that Gary was the type who would not talk to a policeman unless he had to.

"Okay, come on in. I'll answer your questions if I can."

"Thanks," Joe said, opening the screen door and entering the house. Gary offered him a seat and Joe began the questioning.

"Just fire away if you would please. Tell me when you met Steve, how long you were friends, some of the things you did together. Anything you could tell me about him may be helpful." Joe coaxed.

"I didn't move to Richmond until I was fourteen," Gary started. "Steve had lived here all his life I reckon. My first day of school here, when I was in the eighth grade, is when I met him. We were both in the same room, both the same age. We started out being real good friends that first day. These little towns are boring so every chance we'd get we would hitchhike over to Lexington to party. By the time we turned sixteen we had started spending more and more time in Lexington. We wouldn't show up in school for two or three weeks at a time. If we did show up, we would be high or drunk. The school didn't put up with that for long and we were kicked out." Gary paused momentarily, looking around the room until he found a package of cigarettes. Finding the cigarettes, he lit one and continued.

"For the next four years we did a lot of odd jobs, smoked a lot of dope, and got into trouble with the law. Most of the trouble could have been avoided if we had not been high."

Joe interrupted at this point, "Did you and Steve ever run with a gang?"

"Well, it wasn't really a gang. There were four or five of us guys who were pretty tight. We only ran around together for about a year or so. I haven't heard from any of them except Steve for over ten years. Steve left here when he was twenty. He told me later that he had worked his way down to

Nashville." Gary paused again, then walking into the kitchen he said, "Would you like a beer?"

"Sure, thanks." Joe thought, I would rather have Jack Daniel's, but a beer will do.

Gary came back into the room, opened two cans of Budweiser and handed Joe one. He returned to his chair, made himself comfortable, then he continued.

"Well, two years ago Steve came back to town. He had changed his name to Stoker. He was doing well financially but he was hooked on coke pretty bad at the time. Steve offered me a job working with his road crew. I accepted it, which I probably should not have done."

"Why is that?" Joe took another gulp of the Budweiser.

"Steve had changed more than his name. He would throw fits if things weren't exactly the way he wanted them. I had seen him get pretty high lots of times, but I had never seen him so inconsiderate. I left him about six months before he was killed." Gary was finished.

"What do you know about Steve's relationship with Carla?" Joe asked. He was becoming more interested in Gary's story now.

"That was a mess. Carla come back here with Steve. They were telling everyone they were going to be married. When I got to Nashville, I never saw them together, except at the studio and they were not alone then. Carla works for Susan Jordon. Susan used to be Steve's manager or some damned thing." Gary stopped again.

"What about Susan, did she have a thing for Steve?" Joe took advantage of the silence.

"She was the boss, man. She played the part to the max. This upset Steve and that's why he always tried to irritate her. Susan was the only person I ever saw that could jump in Steve's shit and get away with it. Once, when Steve was talking to Carla at the recording studio, Susan blew up. She was so pissed off that she threatened to kill Steve if he so much as looked at Carla again." Gary finished his beer, got up from the chair and returned to the kitchen for another one. "You want another beer?" He asked.

"No thanks, I have a long drive ahead of me. If you don't have anything else to add, then I will be leaving." Joe got up from his seat. Gary followed him to the door.

"I sure hope I cleared up your questions about Steve's claim."

Back in the Toyota, Joe made notes on all that he had learned here in Richmond. It was 10:00 P.M. when he finished making the entries in his notebook. Putting the car in gear and easing into the light traffic, Joe was Nashville bound.

Out of habit Joe kept the Toyota in the southbound lane. He could not see the road in front of him, his mind was preoccupied with the Stoker homicide. Joe thought, Steve Cranston had a past-twenty years of past. Steve Stoker's past had only been a short nine years. Cranston nor Stoker would ever have a future. They had both ceased to exist at the same instant, on stage at the silver Horse café in Dallas, Texas.

Chapter Seven
Now Appearing at the Nashville City Morgue

It began to rain about sixty miles from Nashville. Joe turned the wipers on. He wasn't tired but he was getting drowsy. It was time for coffee. He stopped at the next truck stop, by then the rain had eased some. Joe needed time to sort out the events of the past week. The only thing he had been able to determine as fact was that a twenty-nine-year-old male singer had been killed.

Joe took a seat in a corner booth. There was hardly anyone in the restaurant. In a few minutes the waitress took his order. She had been sitting in the back of the establishment, talking with some truck drivers and did not seem to be overly pleased about having her conversation interrupted.

"A pot of black coffee please," Joe said, politely. She made it more obvious that she had not enjoyed serving Joe. She was cute but she could use a personality improvement or, as they say an attitude adjustment.

When the friendly waitress had left the table, Joe pulled a napkin from its holder and started to list a few things he had to do the next day in Nashville;

1. *Call Miller*

2. *Gain Carla's confidence, must find out what she knows*

3. *Do some research on Susan!!!*

4. *Locate Denny Deal*

5. *Return the Toyota to the rental office*

The coffee was being placed on the table by the friendly waitress. He couldn't think of anything else to add to the list, so Joe folded it twice and placed it in his shirt pocket. He smiled at the waitress to indicate to her that her foul mood was not affecting him in the least. She did not return the smile.

The coffee had been black, hot and strong. Just what he had needed to wake him up. Joe was back in the Toyota and wide awake. The rain had resumed, more heavily than before. Joe turned the radio on and tuned in a Nashville station.

"We interrupt this program to bring you a special news

bulletin. A young singer has been found dead at his

Nashville apartment. His identity is being with-held

until next of kin is notified. Nashville police suspect

murder!!"

The announcer made the headlines sound like a preview for a movie, Joe thought.

The Nashville skyline was visible ten miles away. It was 2:00 A.M., the bars would be closed. Joe was not disappointed; he knew he had a bottle of Jack Daniel's back at his motel room. There was very little traffic when Joe took the exit off Interstate 40. He was at his motel within ten minutes. As he opened the door to his room, he noticed a paper lying on the floor. Joe bent over and picked the paper up. The note read;

PLEASE CALL ME WHEN YOU RETURN. THE TIME DOESN'T MATTER. Signed-Carla.

Carla must have been a light sleeper, thought Joe. She answered the phone on the second ring.

"Hello," the sleepy voice was Carla's.

"This is Joe, you wanted me to call?"

"Yes Joe, I'm scared. I found Denny Deal dead in his apartment this morning. I think Susan knows something about it."

Well, he thought, that takes care of two items on my list-I won't have to bother with locating Denny Deal and Carla's confidence has been established. Joe broke the silence. "We will have lunch tomorrow, we can discuss it then, okay?"

"Sure Joe, goodnight." Carla sounded frightened but relieved.

Joe did not bother with a glass, he opened the bottle of Jack Daniel's and placed it directly to his lips. Tomorrow will be a long day, he thought as he lay back on the bed and closed his tired eyes. He didn't know how long he lay there because when he got up, he didn't bother to check the time. He took a couple more swigs of straight Jack Daniel's and started to write songs. As he wrote he realized this music business was only temporary for him. Although he had enjoyed the excitement, he knew that he was a dedicated policeman and would soon be returning to the reality of the policeman's world.

At 8:00 A.M. Joe was out of bed and on the telephone, talking to Captain Miller. "I may need you to verify that I am a police officer. There has been a murder here in Nashville. I think the victim was involved in the Stoker homicide. I'm going to need some info from the PD here. If they call to verify my identity, help me out." Joe then briefed his Captain on the successful trip to Richmond. Miller sounded pleased to have something substantial to report to Chief Reynolds.

"Good work Joe. Don't let up now and stay off the booze." Miller didn't mind letting Joe know when he did good police work.

"I'll only call when I have something to report," said Joe.

At 612 Magnolia, Joe parked in the drive and walked to the entrance. Out of habit he almost rang the doorbell then he reached for the handle and pushed the door open, unannounced. As he walked into the office entrance, he startled Carla, who seemed to be extremely jumpy this morning. When she saw that it was Joe, she became more relaxed. "Damn I'm glad it's you. Susan's out at the moment, we're alone so we can talk."

Joe tried not to let his impatience show, "What has you so damned upset this morning?"

Carla checked outside to make sure no one was in the drive then she began to talk. "I started working for Susan about four years ago. That was right after Steve showed up here. Then Denny Deal started hanging around here a lot after Steve's death. Now the same thing is happening with you. I don't have to remind you that Steve and Denny are both dead now. I'm worried about you Joe."

"There's no reason for you to worry about me, I can handle myself." Joe embraced Carla, kissing the top of her head.

She looked up at Joe and continued her account of what she knew about Susan. "Why, I'm not sure, but everyone she has anything to do with mysteriously ends up dead. After Steve was killed, I became frightened."

"Why is that?" Joe was brief with his questions; he didn't want to sidetrack Carla while she was on a roll.

"I had gone home one evening, just before Steve's death. When I had driven about halfway home, I realized that I had forgotten something here at the office. When I returned Susan and Steve were in the recording studio. I heard shouting, then as the studio door opened, I saw Steve walk out into the hallway. Susan was screaming and threw an ashtray at him. She was obviously very upset. She threatened to kill Steve. One week later he was dead."

"Do you think she did it?" Joe asked.

"I can't be sure," Carla replied. "Two days ago, while you were in the recording studio, Denny called the office. Susan took the call out here at the desk. I only heard one side of the conversation but that was enough to know it concerned money that Denny owed her. Susan raised her voice as she told

Denny, 'You're through in the music industry, you son-of-a-bitch.'" Carla began to weep. "What am I going to do Joe?"

Joe thought for a moment, holding Carla in his arms. It was now or never he thought. I'm going to stop the charades; this investigation is getting stale anyway.

"Carla I'm about to tell you something you may not like. Before I tell you, I want to say that if you are involved in these murders, I will try to help you any way I can, legally." Carla pulled away from Joe, giving him a confused glance.

"You see," he said, "I'm a police officer. I'm here on assignment from Dallas. I could have gone on pretending to be a good ole boy, trying to get into the music business but I think it's best that I tell you the truth."

Carla slumped down until she was sitting on the edge of the desk. "Am I in trouble?"

"I don't think so, unless you are directly involved or have been hiding evidence. I do need your cooperation and perhaps you could assist me in solving this mystery," said Joe.

"I'll do anything I can to help. Just tell me what you want me to do."

"Did you go to Kentucky with Steve two years ago?' Joe started to question her to determine how honest she was going to be with him. Carla acted surprised that Joe knew about her and Steve, but she answered correctly.

"Yes, I did. Susan found out and she fired me for it. She hired me right back the following week. She apologized for taking her frustrations out on me. I knew it was because she had been in love with Steve. I can't explain why I even went to Kentucky with him. I guess we all do crazy things now and then. When I learned that Steve had been killed, I confronted Susan about it. About Steve's death. She knew that I suspected her. She told me to mind my own business or I may find myself seeking new employment. I was indebted to Susan then as I still am today. She makes sure that all of her employees owe her. It gives her a feeling of security; she likes

to own people. I have wanted to leave but feared for my life."
Carla had kept rattling on at such a pace that Joe had not
found an opening to insert a question. She pretty well told all
she knew though.

Carla had given a description of an inhuman monster,
capable of violence and other unlawful acts. Joe asked Carla
to find out all she could about Susan's previous marriage and
the cause of Carlton Jordon's death.

"I'll check the Nashville PD and get the run down on
Denny," said Joe.

He'd had to confide in someone sooner or later. There
was just too much ground for one man to cover. If Carla was
sincere, she would be a great asset to Joe. If she was lying,
and there were some lying ladies, Joe would be sorry he had
revealed his reasons for his presence here in Nashville.

After two or three phone calls to the Dallas police
department the stooping, gray haired old sergeant at the desk
was convinced that Joe was who he claimed to be. Joe was
given a police pass and directed to the plain clothes
detective's office.

He knocked on the door for courtesy and stepped inside
the smoky room. After he had explained why he was there one
of the detectives, and huge man, got Denny's case folder from
the filing cabinet and gave it to Joe.

"Ain't much here yet," he said. "Maybe you can help us
with it."

Joe quickly read the thin file. A simple and clean murder,
assassin style. What a coincidence. This homicide was very
similar to the Stoker homicide. Two fatal gunshot wounds to
the head. The ballistics reports would be complete the next
day. Joe made a note to have Captain Miller mail the ballistics
reports from the Stoker homicide. It was a hunch, but Joe's
imagination was a vast one.

What a day it has been, thought Joe. He had been busier
than a one-legged man at an ass-kicking contest. He had

returned the Toyota to the rental office and had returned to his motel room by taxi. Once he was safely inside his room, he found his bottle of Jack Daniel's, what was left of it, and carried it over to the bed. Taking several long swigs of the good whiskey Joe dialed the long-distance directory assistance.

"What city?"

"Dallas," he answered.

"May I help you?" the operator asked.

"The Torn Dollar Saloon please," Joe waited while the operator searched for the number. The phone rang several times then Joe distinguished Julie's voice.

"Hi Julie, it's Joe! I have been intending to call but I have been stuck in Nashville on police matters." Joe explained.

"Joe, I thought I would never hear from you again." Julie sounded surprised.

"Could I see you when I get back to Dallas?" Joe asked anxiously.

"I'll be right here at the Torn Dollar, as usual." Joe detected boredom in her voice now.

When Joe hung up, he checked his Timex. Thirty-five minutes. He never talked that long. He usually kept his phone conversations brief. He must really have some affection for Julie. He was never certain of his feelings for women.

Joe was certain of one thing-Denny Deal would never do another live performance in Nashville. Tonight, Denny would be appearing dead, at the Nashville city morgue...

Chapter Eight
Lying Ladies

Joe was about to leave his motel room when the phone started to ring. He stopped at the door and looked at the phone as if he were trying to decide if he should answer it or let it ring. The caller persisted. After eight rings he picked up the receiver. It could be something important.

"This is Joe," he answered.

"Joe, I'm glad I caught you in." It was Susan. "Do you have plans for the evening?" She asked.

"What did you have in mind?" He answered Susan's question with a question of his own.

"I have reservations for two at Phil's, are you interested?"

Joe accepted her invitation, letting her know that he did not have transportation. Susan told him to be ready in fifteen minutes and she would pick him up.

Women, thought Joe, you can't live with them and you can't live without them. He changed his clothes to something more formal than his Wranglers and waited. A few minutes later Susan's Cadillac pulled up in front of the motel. Joe went out and got into the car.

Phil's was not the sort of restaurant Joe would normally frequent. It was too classy. He felt uncomfortable and out of place as the waiter showed them to their table. The tie choked Joe and he felt naked without his boots. He had not worn slippers for a long time.

Susan started the conversation. "Joe I could use a man with your talent to help me run my business. A woman has a difficult time alone. Lots of times people try to take advantage of me." She seemed to be seeking Joe's sympathy.

"Exactly what kind of business are you in?" Joe asked sharply.

"Now what kind of question is that? You know I'm in the publicity business." She glared at Joe contemptuously, her displeasure obvious.

Joe enjoyed the discomfort he was causing her. Adding fuel to the fire he continued with more cutting remarks. "You seem to be doing very well with your solo act. I would hate to spoil your operation." For now, Joe was flatly refusing her offer.

The longer he talked to this selfish woman the more contemptible she became. Joe felt that Susan had been deceiving him about one thing or another since he had first met her. He gave her credit; she was a skillful liar.

Joe continued to make small talk with Susan as he suffered through dinner. She drove him back to his motel at about 11:00 P.M. He did not wish to completely spoil her evening, so Joe promised to give her offer some consideration. He had no intentions of giving it further thought.

He could not wait to get inside, as he got out of the car, he quickly removed the tie. Later, dressed in his Wranglers and a tee shirt, Joe located his songwriting tools and began to write. He had been thinking about the lyrics to a song all during dinner. Susan had inspired this one;

> Lying ladies, lying ladies
> Tell you that they care
> Lying Ladies drive you crazy
> Lying ladies are everywhere
> Beware of angels that act like devils
> When they hold you in their arms
> When they speak softly then you're in trouble
> Cause you're captured by their charms
> Keep your eyes open don't you stop hopin'
> That you'll find one that does not lie
> You may never find one who's always honest
> But don't give up you've got to try
> Some make their own beds, but they won't lie there
> They'd rather lie with someone new
> They'll mislead you until they leave you

Then you'll have no one to lie with you

The phone rang. It was Carla. "Joe, I have the information you asked for. I was going through Susan's desk and found several newspaper clippings about her husband's death. Carlton Jordon died, listen to this, from two fatal gunshot wounds! He was shot in the head! The article goes on to say the murder weapon was a .38 caliber handgun. It was never discovered, naturally." Carla was excited.

Joe's head was spinning now. A shot of Jack Daniel's would solve that. Joe opened the bottle and swallowed the remaining contents. Throwing the empty bottle at the trash can and missing, he said, "When was he killed Carla?"

"I don't remember the exact day, but it was sometime in September seventy-nine. That was just before I was employed by Susan. Why do you suppose she never talked about her husband Joe?" Carla asked, innocently.

"I don't know Carla, I just don't know," Joe sighed.

Joe was baffled. He had been assigned to tougher cases, but it had been a long time since he had not been able to uncover enough evidence to question a real suspect. It wasn't that he was lacking for suspects, the problem was having too many clues thrown at him. He would have to decipher all of his notes and hopefully come up with something soon.

If he could discover one piece of hard evidence to lead him in the right direction, he could have the case solved in a matter of days. This one piece of evidence was waiting for Joe at Denny Deal's apartment. All Joe had to do was find it.

Joe could not sleep though he desperately needed to. He checked his notes again and again for that one clue he may have overlooked. What the hell, he thought, as he was getting dressed. This case is not going to solve itself. I'll have to get out there on the street.

He called a taxi and waited for it in the parking lot. When the cab arrived, Joe slid into the front seat.

"Take me to 1665 West 31st street," he told the driver. The taxi stopped about thirty minutes later in front of a three-story brick building.

It was a clean neighborhood. Joe observed. But definitely middle class. Joe walked into the lobby of the apartment building and up the stairs to apartment 2C. Denny would not be there but just to be sure that no one else was Joe knocked several times. When there was no response, he removed his driver's license from his wallet and let himself into the apartment.

It may have been a middle-class neighborhood, Joe thought, but Denny had been living high on the hog. Everything in the apartment was neatly arranged. There was a well-stocked musical library that filled one complete wall. Joe was impressed.

In one corner of the room there were three microphones, a Fender guitar on its stand, and amplifying unit and two humongous audio speakers. Behind all this was a complete set of drums. Joe continued to walk slowly through the apartment, inspecting. He stopped at the first bedroom.

Pushing open the door and peeking inside Joe saw that in this room too, everything was orderly. In a small room off from the bathroom, Joe found that Denny Deal had interests other than music. He found himself walking into a compact, but professionally equipped dark room. Joe started to search through the doors of the cabinets, not looking for anything specifically.

Several minutes had gone by. He had found absolutely nothing that remotely resembled a clue. There were several prints in manila portfolios. The faces of the models meant nothing to Joe. Most of the prints were of gorgeous ladies under-dressed in skimpy swim wear.

Joe was about to give up on finding anything when a 35mm Pentax that was lying on the worktable caught his eye, the lens cover was missing from the camera. No professional photographer would forget to protect his lens, thought Joe.

Joe walked out of the dark-room and into the back bedroom. Everything in this room too, was disgustingly clean, except for the blood on the carpet and walls. Near the window a chalk outline had been drawn on the floor presumedly by Nashville homicide detectives. The outline indicated the position in which Denny's corpse had been found.

He studied the crime scene carefully. Joe noted the messy scraps of bones and blood that had splattered on the walls and curtain. A dark colored object drew his attention. The object was lying, partially hidden by the curtain, which was too long for the window. He walked over to the window, stooped and picked the circular piece of plastic up from the floor. It was the missing lens cover.

Joe peered out the window. The view wasn't the greatest, just a paved parking lot below. He returned to the dark room with the lens cover. Picking the camera up to replace the lens cover, Joe noticed the infrared lens and the roll of film which had not been removed from the Pentax. Joe thought, maybe, just maybe Denny had been using the camera at the time of his murder.

Joe turned the red lights on, and the bright overhead lights shut off automatically. I'll develop this roll and see what caught Denny's interest, he thought, hoping he could remember all the procedures for developing the film.

He removed the roll of film from the Pentax and started to unwind the spool. Taking the film to the developing tank, he placed it on one of the reels. He then dropped the reel into the solution, closed the door to the tank and set the timer for twenty minutes.

"Time for a drink," Joe said aloud.

When he had entered the apartment, Joe had noticed a small wet bar in the front room. He went to the bar and searched under the counter hoping to find a bottle of Jack Daniel's. Not finding his favorite whiskey. He settled on a bottle of Jim Beam instead. Unscrewing the top, Joe poured about three fingers into a glass. He got ice and a cola from the fridge and once again returned to the dark room.

A few minutes later the timer sounded. Joe removed the negatives from the tank and took them to the wet table. He checked the negatives by holding them in front of a high intensity lamp. They appeared to be okay. While the negatives were drying, Joe searched around the room. He found the drawer marked, 'PRINGING PAPER'. He removed a package from the drawer and placed an 8x10 inch piece of the paper under the enlarger. Then placing a dry negative in the guide, he turned the enlarger on. Three minutes later he had the print soaking in the final solution. Joe followed the same procedure with the ten remaining negatives.

After the prints were ready Joe turned the red light off. Looking at the pictures he thought, models, nothing but models. Wait a minute. What is this? He stared closer at one of the prints. A picture of Susan. Observing the background Joe noted the picture had been taken at Denny's apartment. Then another print caught his eye. Carla? Sitting at the bar in Denny's front room. It was a recent photograph for she wore the same short, yellow skirt Joe had admired the day he had made the recording. That had been the same night Denny had been killed.

The last picture bothered Joe; it was blurry. It appeared to have been taken from the bedroom window. The woman's face was not visible, but Joe would have sworn under oath that he knew her. In the photograph there were several cars parked in the parking lot. Joe estimated the picture had been taken with the infrared lens at about the time of Denny's death, midnight, he remembered from the homicide report.

Joe was about to put the photograph away when it suddenly came to him why the woman had looked so familiar. It was that purse, that damned purse. It was uniquely designed, and Joe knew that he had seen that purse before. But where?

Joe was concerned now about revealing his identity to Carla. Maybe she was not being perfectly honest with him.

She had put on a good act about being frightened of Susan. If she was so frightened then why had she been socializing with her, here at Denny's apartment? Joe's investigative blood was boiling now.

He was going to get some straight answers that he wanted to hear. Screw these lying ladies and their prefabricated bullshit. But first he was going after that cold, hard evidence. Lay real evidence in a criminal's lap and they have no place to crawl. Some confess but others hold on till the very end. Joe's imagination was uncontrollable now.

It was 4:00 A.M. when he arrived at his motel room. This time when he lay down, he could sleep, Joe was exhausted. He slept until noon the next day. If he had dreamed, he did not recall any part of it.

Very rarely did Joe eat breakfast but this morning, or afternoon, he was starving. He showered, dressed and walked to the motel restaurant. He ate an omelet with grits, drank a pot of coffee, then ordered pancakes and syrup.

After Joe had finished his feast he called for a taxi, then returned to his table where he waited for the cab to arrive. When he saw the cab pull up in front of his room he rushed out of the restaurant. He told the little black lady who was driving the cab, "Take me to the police station please."

The cab driver made Joe extremely uncomfortable. Her foot was glued to the brake pedal all the way to the police station. When she stopped in front of the building Joe was relieved to get out of the taxi. The meter read $6.00. "Keep the change," he told her, handing her a $10.00 bill.

He hurried inside. The same sergeant from the previous day was at the desk. He recognized Joe and did not demand him to go through the identification routine again. The sergeant handed Joe a police pass, and Joe went in to chat with the detectives. He wanted to check to see if there had been any new developments on the Denny Deal case.

"Have you gotten anything on this Deal mess yet?" One of the detectives asked Joe.

"Not really anything on the Deal case, but I'm following up on a hunch I have on the Stoker case. Of course, it could tie in. Who can say how these things will turn out?"

"You got that shit right," said another detective. "Once me and Ray had a case where a man had killed his friend. It had been and accident, but the man got so scared that he tried to make it appear to be a murder. We never seen so many clues in one case, did we Ray?"

Ray, a young policeman, about twenty-six, six feet tall with dark hair and a dark complexion, stood up and walked around the room. Ray appeared to be restraining his energy, uncomfortably trapped in a small room like the one the detectives were in presently. Finally, Ray stopped pacing and spoke.

"Man, I was getting calls in the middle of the night, at home, from this jerk. He was giving me so many leads that I could not check them all. If he would have just confessed, he would have been cleared. But as it turned out he got charged with murder one. He had left so much fake evidence on the scene the real evidence could not validate his alleged accident story in court. The judge burned his ass. He's probably still in the joint." Ray finished.

Joe thought, it sure is good to hear these real-life comedies that only a policeman can tell.

"Anyway," Joe said, to no one specific, "I came by to see if we could dig in the files for a Jordon homicide. It happened sometime in September 1979."

"Was the case ever solved?" Ray wanted to know.

"I don't think it was," said Joe.

Ray got up from his chair again and said, "Come with me." Joe followed Ray out of the detective's squad room and down the corridor to the records room.

"There you are Joe," said Ray as he opened the door and made a gesture for Joe to enter the room. "Help yourself. If it happened in seventy-nine it is probably just as buried as Jordon himself." Ray laughed as he left Joe alone in the records cemetery.

Sifting through the records Joe stopped to read some of the more interesting ones. Just before he reached the '79 pile, he was still in 1980, he found a case that aroused his curiosity. Joe read the first page. The synopsis read;

Kenneth Russell, a twenty-one-year old white male was the victim of an overdose of drugs (identified as cocaine by crime lab-see attached report) All indications are that the drug was not self- administered, However, all efforts to develop sufficient evidence met with negative results. The wife of the deceased, Carla Russell, was arrested and questioned. Failing to obtain evidence in this investigation, this department was forced to release Carla. No charges have been filed at present. Due to the lack of investigative leads this case is closed, to be reopened in the event new leads or evidence should develop...

Joe put the folder aside. This rates further research, he thought. At last he located the Jordon folder. He placed all the records neatly in stacks and, carrying the two folders with him, he returned to the detective's squad room.

Joe sat at a desk and thoroughly read each line of every page of the Jordon file. Carla was a lying lady; Joe was convinced of that much. But she had not lied about Jordon's death. He had been shot twice in the head. The murder weapon, a .38 caliber handgun, had not been discovered. This case too, had been placed in the suspense files, pending development of evidence.

Susan Jordon had not been suspected as she had presented an alibi. It was airtight according to the police report, which did not surprise Joe. She always came out clean. Joe had suspected Susan for various reasons, but she always seemed to escape. She never left a single shred of evidence that could be used against her.

Joe asked Ray to keep the two case folders handy. "I think I am going to be using them again before too long." He sounded hopeful. "Could you guys send an official request to the Dallas PD? Ask them for the ballistics report from the Stoker homicide. I'll need to compare them with the report on the Deal case. If they match, then I'll have a good hunch in what direction to start looking."

"Sure, we'll be glad to help," said Ray.

As Joe was leaving, he made one last statement, "Ray, be careful on these Nashville streets. There are some lying ladies running loose."

Chapter Nine
What Are Friends For?

June 3, 1980 was a hot day in Nashville. For the fortunate ones who could afford air conditioning the heat was bearable. At 7:00 A.M. the alarm went off. Carla Russell reached across Kenny to silence it. He had slept through the noise of the alarm clock. When she called his name, he did not respond. He would lose this job as he had lost all the others.

They had only been married for three years and already he had been through at least a dozen different jobs. Carla thought, this is it. I've had it with this way of life. The bed was soaking wet, the pungent odor of perspiration nauseating. She had just washed the sheets the previous day at the laundry on the corner.

As Carla glanced around the sparsely furnished, two room apartment she decided that she would escape this lazy son-of-a-bitch. One way or another she would not spend another night in this dump. She did not bother trying to wake Kenny again.

She would have liked to had breakfast but there hadn't been any groceries in the apartment in over a month. A whole damned month. That's when Kenny had lost his last job. He had just started to work again yesterday. It was temporary work, but the pay was supposed to be good. Kenny had been elated when he came home last night. He had told Carla how some real nice lady, over on Magnolia, had given him a job as an audio technician. He was going to be working at a recording studio.

Kenny Russell had been one of the top audio men in the business. He'd had a bright future at the age of nineteen. That was before drugs had become more important to him than keeping a job. He had been fired by musicians all over Nashville. Mostly for not showing up for work.

Carla searched through Kenny's wallet until she found the business card. Maybe I should go by the recording studio to let them know that Kenny won't be in today, she thought. She quickly dressed in her one and only decent looking dress, left the apartment and walked outside into the unbearable heat.

She walked down the street to the phone booth and started to dial the number from the business card. When Carla saw the taxi, she quickly replaced the phone to its hook and hailed the taxi. She gave the driver the address and twenty minutes later the cabbie dropped her off at 612 Magnolia street.

As she walked up to the house Carla admired the interesting structure. She almost decided to turn and run. Why had she come to this place? It was uncharacteristic of her to act this way. I'll just ring the bell once, if no one answers then I'll leave, she thought.

She rang the bell, waited a few seconds, then turned to leave. As she turned a young man opened the door. "Hi! Could I help you?" He asked.

At first it startled Carla. She was at a loss for words. "Yes, I, aha…aha…, I'm Carla Russell. Is Mrs. Jordon in?" She stammered.

"No, she's out at the moment. But you are welcome to come inside and wait, if you'd like," said the man. He had a very friendly voice.

"okay," she said, "If you're sure it's alright."

"I'm Steve. I work with Mrs. Jordon. You could say she is my manager." He paused for a moment, staring admiringly at Carla, them he asked, "What brings a cute little thing like you out so early in the morning?"

"My husband just got a job here yesterday. He's working in the recording studio." Carla was shy.

"Oh yea, I remember the new guy, Kenny wasn't it?" Steve asked.

"Yes. Why I really came here was to let someone know that Kenny won't be able to make it to work today. I tried to get him up this morning, but he won't wake up. I'm afraid he will lose this job." Carla rushed through her explanation then started to cry.

"Well Mrs. Jordon doesn't like for anyone to be late, that's for sure. Say, maybe I could help. Let's go to your place and I'll try to wake Kenny." Steve offered.

Carla agreed to the offer. Outside in the driveway, Carla watched as Steve opened the garage door and backed the maroon Corvette out onto the pavement. He got out of the car, closed the garage door and opened the passenger door for Carla. This is style, she thought. Why can't Kenny be a gentleman like this sometime. Carla rested her head on the plush seat and enjoyed the short ride to her apartment.

Inside the tiny apartment Kenny was still soundly sleeping in the sweat soaked bed. Steve shook him several times. Finally, he stirred. Half awake, Kenny said "What the fuck's going on?"

Steve pulled him into a sitting position. "What kind of shit is he on?" Steve asked Carla.

"I have no idea," she said.

Steve picked the groggy Kenny up, draped him over his shoulder and carried the drugged man to the shower. After sitting Kenny on the floor of the shower Steve turned the cold water on as high as it would go. Kenny woke up in a rage.

"Who in the hell are you?" Kenny asked when he saw Steve.

"I'm Steve. You're supposed to be doing some audio work on my album today. Get the lead out. I'll wait for you." Steve left the soaked Kenny staring blankly up into the cold shower spray.

Carla was impressed at the way Steve had so coolly handled the situation. In the kitchen, when their eyes met,

Carla attempted a smile. "I'd like to offer you coffee or something but I'm afraid poverty prevents that right now."

"I understand," Steve said, compassionately.

Ten minutes later both men were leaving the apartment. Steve said goodbye to Carla. Kenny glared at her on his way out the door. Carla reflected on the recent scene that had just occurred. Steve could probably handle any situation. She admired a man that could take control.

She removed the soaked sheets from the bed. With only two sets of linen Carla had to do the laundry every other day. It had been that way all summer. The repetitious task was driving her batty. If Kenny could keep this job, maybe they could recover from the slump they were in.

Shortly after noon Carla heard the knock on the door. Now who could that be? She thought. No one had ever been to their apartment that she could remember. She opened the door and was pleasantly surprised to see Steve standing in the hallway.

"What are you doing here?" She demanded; her surprise evident.

"I thought I would stop by and take a beautiful lady to lunch," Steve said.

"Why are you doing this?" Carla asked, suspiciously.

"What are friends for?" asked Steve. "Will you join me?" Carla was hesitant in answering. Then she thought, what could it possibly hurt? "Okay Steve, I'll have lunch with you, but only as a friend." She warned.

"That's all I had in mind," promised Steve.

Lunch went very well. Maybe Steve's intentions had been perfectly respectable. Maybe he had just wanted to offer Carla some mental support, cheer her up. She had been so depressed that morning. Whatever his intentions had been Carla was glad that she had accepted his invitation.

Every day for the next week Steve and Carla had lunch together at the same restaurant. Surprisingly, Carla thought, nothing immoral had happened between them. She knew that if Steve had made advances she would have submitted. She was relaxed with Steve. Maybe he had just wanted to be her friend. He was certainly the most understanding man Carla had ever met.

Carla described the precarious marriage she was going through. How she was becoming tired of Kenny being unable to keep a job. How she expected more out of life than a shabby, two room apartment and two sets of linen that she could see through. Steve had listened patiently to all of her problems.

Three weeks had gone by since Kenny had started the job at 612 Magnolia. He was drying out and seemed to be on the road to complete recovery. He had abstained from drugs and had promised Carla that he would never become involved with drugs again. In short, Kenny Russell had cleaned up his act. Usually he would be awake before the alarm clock would go off. He would have showered and dressed before Carla had opened her eyes. For the last three weeks Kenny Russell had probably been the best damned husband any woman could have asked for. He was considerate and loving. Carla regretted ever thinking about leaving him.

Shocked? Hell yes, Carla was shocked. When the alarm went off at 7:00 A.M., June 24, 1980, she reached across Kenny's cold body to silence the alarm. She called Kenny's name several times. He did not respond. She shook him but he did not move.

At first Carla was angry then she touched his shoulder. As she felt the cold skin against her fingers, her anger turned to fear then to panic. Kenny would not be going to work today or ever again for that matter. Sometime during the night Kenny Russell had taken his last breath.

Carla quickly dressed and ran from the apartment. And ran down the street to the phone booth and dialed 911, the police emergency number. "He's dead!" She screamed hysterically.

"Calm down lady, who's dead?" Asked the desk clerk at the Nashville police station.

After a few minutes had passed Carla had calmed down enough to give the clerk her address. She slowly returned to the apartment, stopping at the door. "I can't go in there," she mumbled. "I can't be alone in there with Kenny's dead body." She sat on the floor in the hallway and waited for the police to arrive.

She felt as though hours had passed but Carla had only been sitting there ten minutes when the young uniformed officer offered her his hand. The policeman helped her to stand. She was not crying but was in a stupor. She followed the two policemen into the apartment and dropped into a straight-backed chair at the small table.

Carla closed her eyes as the older policeman checked Kenny's body for vital signs. She closed her eyes tighter when she heard him say to his partner, "Yea, he's dead alright. Better get on the Motorola, Bill, and call the station. Get the dicks out here. Have the station to get an ambulance and call the coroner's office."

"Right Jack," the young patrolman acknowledged.

In a matter of minutes, the tiny apartment was filled with uniformed policemen, plainclothes detectives and other officials. The ambulance had arrived, and the two paramedics waited impatiently until the coroner had pronounced Kenny Russell dead. The body was quickly covered and removed from the room.

Carla still had not moved from her seat at the table. Nor had she uttered a single word. She just stared in disbelief at the activity taking place in the crowded apartment.

"Mrs. Russell." Carla did not respond.

"Mrs. Russell!" Jack said again, louder this time. "You will have to accompany us to the police station." She got up from the table when Jack took her by the arm and led her to the police cruiser at the curb outside.

The ride to the police station seemed endless, Carla was thinking, as the young patrolman wheeled the police cruiser into the police parking lot. She was taken inside and told to have a seat in one of the interview rooms. "Someone will be with you shortly," said Jack.

Half an hour later a plainclothes detective entered the room. "Mrs. Russell? I'm Sergeant Stindish and I must ask you some questions. I know this is not a very good time, but these things won't wait." Stindish was very kind.

The preliminary questioning took several minutes.

"Did you know Kenny used drugs?"

"What drugs did he use most frequently?"

"What time did you last see your husband alive?"

They were routine questions which Carla answered truthfully.

When Sergeant Stindish had exhausted his list of standard questions he said, "You may go now. Just be available in the event further questioning becomes necessary."

Carla returned to her apartment by taxi. She hurriedly packed one piece of luggage and left the rest of her miserable world behind. She did not even look behind her as she closed the door. Outside, she inanely checked the mailbox one last time. One envelope with no postmark, addressed to Carla Russell. She nervously tore open the envelope and unfolded the single sheet of stationery. What she read chilled her to the bone. She read the words aloud, "You're free now. What are friends for?"

Chapter Ten
The Purse

Four Nashville specimens and two Dallas specimens. All fragments of bullets which had been removed from the brain tissue of three murder victims. Joe checked with the detectives at the Nashville police station. "Did the ballistics report arrive from Dallas yet?" He was anxious.

"Yea, I think it just got here," a short detective named Barney told him.

Joe found the package, opened it and after studiously looking over the report, sighed, "Barney I don't know shit about this scientific crap. I think I'll ride over to the crime lab and let someone there tell me what this report means. Want to come along?"

"Sure, I'll get a car and pick you up out front." Barney took the hint.

When Joe and Barney got to the police crime lab, they were escorted by one of the lab technicians. He was a nervous little man, with a twitch that made Barney shudder.

"Could I assist you gentlemen?" Igor asked, reminding Joe of the doctor's assistant in the movie Frankenstein.

"Yea, I would like to know all you can tell me about this ballistics report," Joe said, handing Igor the folder.

Igor took the folder from Joe and quickly scanned its contents. "Well in this type of case, where there is no suspected murder weapon, ballistics reports can only be filed with the report until a weapon is discovered. Once the weapon is found it will be test-fired. The test-fired specimen will then be microscopically compared with the bullet or bullet fragment found at the scene of the crime." Igor explained the procedure. "Ballistics is a sophisticated area of forensic science which is based on comparison of two or more specimens. A gun can be positively identified by the characteristic marks its rifling makes on a bullet fired from it. We use a technique called periphery photography to record the whole surface of the bullet at once."

Igor Einstein started to continue but Joe interrupted. "Look, can you tell me, by looking at the photographs of the bullets in this case, if they were fired by the same weapon used in another case?" Joe asked.

"Certainly," Igor was brief.

Joe then told him the other two cases would probably be on file there at the crime lab, since they had performed the examination of the evidence obtained in the Jordon and Deal cases.

After checking his files for the Jordon and Deal cases, Igor compared the photographs from all three specimens. "In my professional opinion I would say the same gun, a .38 caliber pistol, fired all of these bullets. You understand that I will have to make a further examination of the photographs to be sure? A suspected murder weapon would also have to be located and test-fired before I could be absolutely positive."

Joe thanked him and left the folder on the Stoker file with Igor, saying, "I'm going to find that weapon."

Barney dropped Joe off at his motel room. Entering the room, Joe remembered that he had drunk the last of his Jack Daniel's. There was a convenient liquor store across the street from the motel. Joe backed out of the room, walked over and returned a few minutes later with three fifths of Jack Daniel's. Opening one of the bottles, he poured a large glass about half full. Now I'm ready to make some phone calls, he thought.

The phone rang twice then Miller answered.

"Captain, I thought I would call to see if I still have a job in Dallas," Joe said, jokingly.

"Hell, I thought you had already quit. I've tried to contact you for the last two days. Where in the hell have you been?" Miller was not in a joking mood.

"I've been investigating Captain," was Joe's answer. Joe filled Miller in on all the events that had occurred since their last contact.

A good stiff drink of Jack Daniel's was what he needed. After his phone conversation with Miller Joe poured a glass full of the Tennessee whiskey, savoring the taste before he swallowed. The drink must have jogged his memory for suddenly he knew exactly where he had seen the purse.

He hurriedly dialed Carla's number, hoping she would be home. It was a little early for she usually did not stop working until 5:00 P.M., two hours from now. Just as he was about to hang up Carla's voice came on the line. "Hello." Joe did not answer; he had not intended to. He pushed the button and made the disconnection.

Step one-Carla is right where he wanted her, now step two. Joe dialed Susan's number. The phone rang twice then the answering machine could be heard. It was Susan's taped voice. He had not expected the answering machine. He could not be sure that the house at 612 Magnolia was unoccupied. He would have to check it out in person.

The taxi stopped in front of Susan's house, Joe got out and made his way quickly to the side of the house. He stayed out of view of anyone passing by on the street in front. He checked the garage; Susan's car was not there. Then he stealthily approached a rear window. A quick inspection revealed an installed alarm system. It was a simple system which Joe deactivated by breaking the circuit. He then climbed, not so gracefully, through the window.

Joe knew what he was looking for as he walked to Susan's bedroom. He opened the closets, checked the drawers, and searched everything in the bedroom, to no avail. He searched the rest of the house and found absolutely nothing. Then finally he entered the recording studio.

Joe employed the same methodical search pattern in the studio that he had used in the house. When he moved an amplifying system that was obstructing the entrance to a closet Joe was pleasantly surprised. The backing fell off the amplifier. When Joe started to replace it, he could not believe he was so fortunate. He returned the amplifier to its original position then practically ran from the studio. He left the house through the same window he had entered, stopping outside to reactivate the alarm system.

His latest discovery had been totally unexpected. The purse was of really no great concern to Joe now, he was still shaking from what he had seen inside the amplifier. But to obtain the evidence legally he would be required to have a search warrant. Joe stopped at a neighborhood bar for a drink, to calm himself. He was still shaking. While he was there, he called Carla.

"I could use a ride, do you mind?" He asked.

"No, I don't mind," said Carla. "Where are you?" Joe checked the book of paper matches lying on the table in front of him, "I'm at a bar called Hogan's. Do you know the place?"

"Sure," she replied, "That's over by Magnolia, I'll be there in a few minutes."

It was closer to an hour when Carla arrived at the bar about 5:00 P.M. Joe was sitting at the bar. As she entered, he saw her and waved. Smiling, Carla joined him.

"Would you like a drink?" Joe asked, hoping she would say yes, because he was ready for another one.

"Martini, dry," she smiled again. Joe ordered their drinks and the two of them moved to a table in the corner.

"The offer you made me the other night; does it still stand?"

"You know it does Joe," Carla sipped her martini.

"Now that you know I'm a police officer, nothing has changed?"

"Not at all," she said. They quickly finished their drinks and left Hogan's bar.

Joe had never been inside Carla's home. He had made it to the front door a few nights earlier. It appeared to be a comfortable place to spend the next few hours. Carla excused herself to go change clothes. While she was out of the room Joe aimlessly wandered around the rest of the house, searching for any type of security system that may have been installed. It may become necessary to burglarize this place in the near future.

Carla returned in a few minutes to find Joe, innocently sitting on the sofa, nursing a Jack Daniel's straight.

"I hope you don't mind," he said, "I helped myself to the whiskey."

"Not at all," said Carla, stepping into the room where Joe could see her more clearly. Now he knew why all of Susan's men had been so attracted to Carla. She wore a skimpy lounging gown that played hide-and-seek with her hardened nipples. The pale beige of the gown accented her dark, tanned skin beneath the garment. The bodice of the gown left little to the imagination. Depending on the motion of her body, and some well-rehearsed positions, he was sure, her firm breasts were completely visible. The situation was becoming sexually intolerable for Joe.

One long zipper was all that protected Carla's modesty. As Joe pinched the zipper between his thumb and forefinger, he did not hear the footsteps behind him. As the zipper moved downward to release those magnificent mounds, Joe leaned forward. He heard Carla's scream but in his sexually aroused condition he was unable to react. Joe felt the sharp pain in his head as someone struck him from behind.

He did not know how long he had been unconscious. When he did muster sufficient strength to sit up the pain was unbearable. Then to add insult and disappointment to his injury, Carla was no longer on the sofa beside him. Joe searched the house for her, but Carla was not here. He checked outside; Carla's yellow Volkswagen was in the drive. At first, he was angry. That bitch set me up, he thought. Joe went back inside and called the police station.

"Detective division please," Joe mumbled into the transmitter. Seconds later Joe recognized Ray's voice.

"Ray Cauley, could I help you?"

"Ray, this is Joe. I would like for you to put an APB out on Carla. I'm not sure of her last name but you can run a make on her car through DMV. The plate number is HN-7574." Joe paused for a moment, wincing at the sharp pain in his head. "I'm not sure where she could be. I was with her at home this afternoon until someone banged me on the head. When I woke up, she was gone." Joe explained the incident to Ray.

The mystery was, who had given him that goose egg on the head? Joe wanted to meet that son-of-a-bitch. He had been actively involved in the Stoker homicide investigation for just over a week. So far, he had stumbled onto three other murders and now this, what was it? A kidnapping? Maybe Carla had just set him up.

He called a taxi and waited for it to arrive. He felt the knot on the base of his skull. The skin had not been broken and the pain was subsiding now. A few minutes later he heard the taxi driver honking the horn. Joe ran outside to the taxi.

It had taken him awhile to get his balance and to see clearly, but by the time the taxi stopped at 612 Magnolia, Joe had regained his composure. Susan's Caddie was parked in the driveway. She never bothered to put it in the garage, Joe thought. He checked the illuminous dial of his Timex. Seven-thirty, shit, thought Joe, I must have been unconscious for more than an hour.

He rang the doorbell and after about five minutes, Susan answered the door. She seemed surprised to see Joe. "Joe," she said, "It's good to see you!"

Joe could sense that he had caught Susan at an inopportune time. She attempted to hide her uneasiness, but it was a weak attempt. "I have some good news Joe. Mr. Wesley called today. He wants to start production on an album tomorrow." She feigned excitement.

Joe did some faking of his own as Susan made small talk for a few moments. She made some excuse to leave the room, walking to the back part of the house. Joe, being a curious creature, followed. He made sure Susan did not see him. She went into one of the guest rooms. Joe could overhear the muffled voices.

"Harry, I can't give it to you tonight. Go on home and I'll see you tomorrow. Now give me a few minutes to get Joe out of the house, I don't want him to see you here. When you hear my car leave then you can go." Susan's voice was distinct. She was an organizer.

Joe had heard enough. He returned to the front office area and was waiting comfortably in a chair when Susan came back into the room.

"Would you like to go have a drink somewhere?" She asked.

"Sure, that would be nice," said Joe, sincerely.

"I'll only be a moment, just have to get my things," she said.

Susan walked out of Joe's sight, into her bedroom. She reappeared seconds later. Smiling a deceptive smile, she said, "Ready when you are."

He had looked right at it as she removed her car keys. He watched her toss it on the car seat as she had gotten into the car. The same one that had fallen to the floor, spilling its contents when he had pulled her into the motel room the first night they had met. He had actually held it in his hand when he had moved it out of the seat to prevent sitting on it. The blow on his head must have affected Joe's memory. He was not thinking properly. How could he have not noticed what he had been searching for earlier that afternoon. It was lying on the seat between he and Susan this very moment. It was the unique turquoise designs that had caused him to remember it in the first place. It was undeniably the purse.

Chapter Eleven
A Vacation for Harry

Harry Fellman was walking the floor. He had been all evening since he had been home. Normally he would have been on the streets. He loved the nightlife and had admitted it to his wife, Margaret, many times. But tonight, was special for Harry, it was his last night as a poor man. He was going to be rich in the morning.

Harry had worked hard all of his life. He was now forty-five, balding and slightly over-weight. For years he had promised to take the wife and kids on a vacation, but something had always come up at the last moment. He had never been able to save enough money. Now the kids were grown but he would still be able to take Margaret.

For the tenth time that evening Margaret Fellman said, "Harry, why don't you sit down? You're driving me crazy, walking the floor." It was all Harry could do to remain silent about his sudden wealth. He didn't have all of the money yet, but tomorrow it would be in his chubby little hands. Then there would be a vacation for Harry.

Finally, he could take it no longer. He kissed Margaret and told her he was going out for a drink. When he first walked into Hogan's bar the place was virtually empty, except for a few of the locals. He didn't notice when Joe and Susan came in around midnight. Harry had been standing at the bar, starting on his sixth gin and tonic.

Susan saw Harry immediately and Joe noticed that she started to act very nervous. "Let's go someplace else. It's dead here," she said.

"Just drop me off at the motel, it's going to be a long day tomorrow," yawned Joe. He was planning his next move before they left the bar.

Susan said goodnight to Joe and sped out of the motel parking lot. Joe did not go inside, instead he called for a taxi from the phone booth near the motel restaurant, sat down on the sidewalk and awaited the arrival of the taxi. The cab arrived and Joe gave the driver the address.

Twenty minutes later the cab was pulling into the curb in front of Hogan's bar. Joe paid the driver, leaving him a small tip, and walked to the entrance of the neighborhood bar. Looking in through the window he could see that Harry was still at the bar.

By now Harry had drunk more than his limit of gin and tonics and his tongue was very loose, thick but loose, nonetheless. He was so excited that he could not keep the secret any longer. Joe bellied up to the bar beside Harry and ordered Jack Daniel's straight.

"That's on me barkeep," Harry slurred. When the bartender set the drink in front of Joe, Harry paid for it with a crisp one-hundred-dollar bill.

If Joe was planning on getting any information from Harry, he had better make his move. It was getting late and Harry was getting tight.

"You must have struck oil mister," said Joe, striking up a conversation.

"No, but I did come into a little money. All I had to do for it was a little favor for this lady friend of mine. Yes sir, I've worked hard all of my life now I'm going to take me a vacation." Harry was obviously more than a little drunk.

"This lady friend of yours, is her name Susan Jordon by any chance?" Joe was taking another wild shot in the dark.

"What do you know about Susan?" Harry asked, sobering somewhat.

"She's a friend of mine." Harry seemed satisfied with Joe's answer as he laughingly said, "Yea, Susan's a real nice lady. She's going to finish paying me in the morning and I'll be on that jet tomorrow night. Me and Margaret are going to Europe or some damned place. I don't really give a shit where we go but we are taking a long-deserved vacation."

The liquor laws state that two o'clock is closing time in Nashville. Joe and Harry were still standing at the bar at ten minutes past two, the clock was intentionally set fast. Harry was weaving and holding onto the bar to keep from falling.

"Drink 'em boys, and we'll see ya'll tomorrow," said the friendly but stern bartender.

It didn't take an investigative mind to solve Harry's performance. Harry, the son-of-a-bitch, had knocked hell out of Joe earlier this evening. Joe wanted to tear his fucking head off but thought, there's time for that later. Harry, the son-of-a-bitch, would also know what had happened to Carla.

It had been Harry Fellman that Susan had been talking to when Joe had gone by her house this evening, after Carla had disappeared. That's why Susan had acted so strangely when she had seen Harry at Hogan's bar tonight. Joe was going to make a special effort to screw up Harry's plans tomorrow. If Joe Ruddy had anything to say about it, there would be no vacation for Harry.

Joe slept really good that night. Maybe it was the bump on the head. He was up early the next morning and on the phone with Ray Cauley. "Ray I need some assistance. I found the bastard that slugged me last night. He's supposed to go for a pay-off this morning." Joe told Ray about his run in with Harry. When he had finished, he asked, "Think you could get an unmarked car and pick me up at the motel?"

"If it means a collar, you can bet your ass I'll be there as soon as I can round up some wheels." Ray was enthusiastic.

After talking to Ray, Joe eyed the three bottles of Jack Daniel's that he had placed on the table the previous day. Could I be an alcoholic? He thought. Here lately he had been drinking more of the amber liquid. Sometimes he drank it even when he didn't want it. What the hell, there's worse things than being an alcoholic. He could be a murderer like someone else here in Nashville.

Ray was ready to go. He was hyper as hell. When Joe slid into the front seat beside him, Ray asked, "Where to Joe, where to?" Joe told him the address, "Six-twelve Magnolia."

They rode quietly until Ray turned the car onto Magnolia street. When Joe had the house in view, he told Ray to park next to the curb, across the street from Susan's house. There they waited for two hours.

Traffic on the street was very light this early in the morning. Joe had counted only three cars passing since they had parked. At 9:15 A.M. a Chevrolet van pulled into the driveway of 612 Magnolia. Joe was about half asleep and didn't see the van.

"Hey Joe, this looks like something getting ready to go down here!" Ray said. Joe shifted in his seat and saw a young man get out of the van. Joe sounded disappointed, "That's not him. Wake me if you see anything else that looks suspicious. I need to catch a little shut eye. I guess I was out on the town too long last night." Joe shut his eyes.

At 10:00 A.M. Joe was awakened by Ray shaking his arm. Joe rubbed his red eyes and said, "That's him Ray!"

They watched as Harry slammed the door of the 1979 Buick. "We'll wait until he leaves then follow him," Joe said. "My guess is, if he gets the money he will go by his place and get Margaret. Then he'll head straight for the airport. If he was not shooting blanks last night, that's exactly what he will do."

Fifteen minutes later Harry reappeared at the door. He was carrying a small attaché case which he did not have when he entered the house. Now Joe was as excited as Ray had been all morning. His hunch had paid off when he had returned to Hogan's bar last night. Harry had been so damned drunk he had not recognized Joe.

Ray was proficient at car tailing. If Harry had noticed them following him, he had not displayed any signs of alarm. It was only a short ride from Susan's to what Joe hoped was Harry's place. Harry parked the Buick in the driveway, and minus the attaché case, he got out of the car and ran into the house.

The front door had barely closed when it opened again. Harry reappeared, burdened by the weight of two large suitcases. He loaded the luggage into the car and made two more trips into the house, returning twice with more luggage.

"This is it," said Joe.

The two detectives waited until Harry and a lady, Joe assumed was Margaret, got into the Buick. Harry backed the big sedan out onto the street. When the Buick started forward Ray followed close behind.

Traffic on the interstate was heavy but Ray handled the tail like a pro. Joe didn't lose sight of the Buick once. The last turn to the airport was just ahead. If all went well for the Fellman's they would be on the plane and in Europe within ten hours. If all went well for Joe and Ray, Harry would be taking a different kind of trip.

When Harry wheeled the Buick into the long-term parking lot Ray followed, flashing his shield at the attendant. The young man waved the policemen through the gate. Harry parked, then unsuspectingly jumped from the Buick. Just as he was about to insert the key into the trunk lock for the luggage, Harry felt the big hand close around his upper arm.

"Planning a trip Harry?" Joe asked.

Harry's knees gave in to the trembling. His wobbling legs could not support the weight of his shaking body. In despair, Harry leaned over the trunk lid and placed his hands behind his back while Ray handcuffed him.

"You have the right to remain silent…" Ray started to read the Miranda warning verbatim from the handy laminated pocket card. All the recruits were issued the cards when they started police academy.

While Ray was handling the technicalities of the arrest Joe walked to the front of the vehicle to inform Mrs. Fellman what was going on. She looked disappointed.

"I should have known that Harry didn't come by all that money honestly. He paced the floor all night last night," she said, disgustedly.

Joe confiscated the attaché case and gave the Buick keys to Margaret. He told her where Harry was being taken so she'd know where to find him later. When Harry was in the car with Joe and Ray, out of Margaret's sight, he started to cry. "One dishonest thing, I knew I shouldn't have done it. I shouldn't have done it." Harry could not control his sobbing.

At the station Harry was booked and charged with abduction. For revenge, Joe threw in the charge of assault and battery. Throughout the booking procedure Harry continued to cry. He was disgustingly cooperative- No, he did not require an attorney: yes, he understood his rights: sure, he would make a statement.

Harry confessed that Susan had hired him to take Carla to an apartment on Jackson Boulevard. He had not been instructed to hurt anyone. Joe had been hurt only because Harry had gotten scared. "I didn't know he was a cop!" Harry cried.

Harry gave the two detectives the address where he had taken Carla. Ray and Joe then counted the money from the attaché case. There was $10,000.00 in one-hundred-dollar bills. Susan must have really wanted Carla out of the picture to pay that kind of money.

As Joe was leaving the station, he saw Harry being led towards the cell block. He would spend the next few weeks there, awaiting trial. With all the evidence poor Harry had against him he would be sentenced to life imprisonment. Assuming that Carla had not been harmed, he may become eligible for parole in about ten years. Joe thought, this is ironic. This is going to be a vacation for Harry.

Chapter Twelve
The Dreaming Kind

It was still early in the afternoon when Joe reached his motel room. He could use some free time; he had been working too hard lately. Joe eyed the bottles of Jack Daniel's as he walked by the table. He was going to do it. Joe was going to make it through a whole day without a drink. It was almost like deserting an old friend. Joe had been with Jack Daniel's for as long as he could remember. Sometimes friends parted too, he thought.

As he was about to step into the shower, he remembered what Susan had said last night. Robert Wesley had wanted to start production on an album today. "Shit," he said, running to the other room to use the phone.

Joe dialed the number and Susan answered.

"Hi Susan, this is Joe. I got tied up and forgot about the album this morning. Did I blow it?" He tried to sound convincing.

"You lucked out Joe. Robert had to leave town, but he does want to see you when he returns. I've tried to contact you all morning."

Joe then explained to Susan that he would be busy for a couple of days. "If you have any messages for me and cannot reach me, leave them with the motel office."

Susan evidently did not suspect that she was being investigated. But based on all that he knew about her, Joe could not believe that she was that dumb. Maybe she knew all about why he was there. Maybe she thought she had covered her tracks so ingeniously that no one could prove her involvement in murder. Well Joe had a surprise for Susan Jordon.

The quick nap that Joe had planned turned into several hours. When he awoke at 3:00 A.M. he felt refreshed. He had been dreaming. Joe had always been the dreaming kind. What puzzled him was that sometimes he could recall all the vivid details of the dreams, then other times only specific portions of them.

This particular dream had been of Julie. He had even seen the red hair, usually he dreamed in color. When he had called Julie's name she would not answer. Then he had tried the name Carla. The redhead quickly turned to face him, she was dressed in a football jersey, the number 17 printed on the front of the garment. It was not Carla's face but that of Julie's.

Although he had acted on hunches conceived from dreams in the past, Joe was not a firm believer in extra sensory perception. Anyway, he did not attempt to understand the dreams. If the hunches paid off Joe passed it off as another lucky guess. Nevertheless, this particular dream bugged him.

The mood for writing songs had escaped Joe for the past few days. He had been so wrapped up in the criminal element of Nashville he had not had time to relax. He wanted a drink of Jack Daniel's but resisted the urge. Instead he opened the desk drawer and removed paper and pen. Fifteen minutes later he had penned this song;

The Dreaming Kind
If you have the time tonight while you're sleeping
Could you let me cross you loving mind again
When you realize the love that you are keeping
I'd be right there to share it all again
I'll meet you every night if you have the time
Though I won't hold your soft warm body next to mine
I'll still love you just as much though we never touch
And you could have me too if you were the dreaming kind
So when you wake up please be reminded
Of the good times we had in your dream
I still love you but babe I was blinded
Now the pretty lady isn't all she seemed
Though we're miles and miles apart in the daytime
I'll see you every night in my sleep
You could see me too if you wanted to be mine

If you were the dreaming kind like me

Joe hummed some melody to the lyrics. It sounded good to him, but it was 3:00 A.M. and he was the only critic.

When Joe had first joined the Dallas police department, a veteran officer named Ted Simpson had told him a story. For some reason Joe thought of that story now.

"Yea Ruddy, you got to make sure when you arrest someone. Make sure they committed the offense," Ted had lectured Joe. "Don't just grab the first piece of evidence you find. Dig around until you have convinced yourself that you are arresting the real criminal. You don't want to make a fool of yourself by arresting someone who just appears to be guilty. A slick prosecutor can convince any jury of a man's guilt but only you should convince yourself that you are making the right arrest. If a police officer doesn't arrest the wrong man, then the jury can't convict the wrong man," Ted warned. He was a philosopher but most of the time his advice was accurate.

"I'll give you an example of what I'm talking about," Ted continued with his story. "One time me and my partner arrested a man that had allegedly raped a young girl. Now we didn't have that much evidence on the man but when the girl picked the poor guy out of a lineup, our emotions took charge. We booked him, dressed the paperwork up some, and charged him with the rape."

Ted stopped talking and seemed to be trying to choose his exact words. Then he started again. "The judge who tried the case had a grudge against the defense attorney, the trial was a joke. The prosecution was allowed to enter all of the evidence against the man. The defense attorney was not allowed to properly represent his client. I felt terrible but it was out of my hands. I could have prevented this one human being from being railroaded by an unfair justice system if I had not been so quick to arrest him." Ted stopped to light a cigarette.

"Well?" Joe asked, "What happened?"

Ted almost had a tear in his eye as he finished his story. "The jury found him guilty and the judge sentenced him to twenty years at Huntsville. Later there was some new evidence found and the real rapist confessed. After my collar had done ten years of his sentence the Governor pardoned him, but he refused to leave the prison. He said his wife would never believe that he had not been the rapist. Anyway, he hung himself in his cell later that night." When Ted finished Joe could see the tears on his cheeks.

"This goddamned cold is kicking my ass," said Ted, as he removed a handkerchief from his hip pocket and wiped his eyes.

Joe wrote another song, using Ted's story as his inspiration;

The Pardon
Ten years ago the judge gave me twenty years
For a crime I knew I never done
Since then I've been just dying here
The victim of a jury that convicted the wrong one
At first you came to visit as often as you could
You swore your love for me would never die
But a number for a lover could never be no good
So reluctantly you told me goodbye
The last time you were here you promised me you'd write
But the mem'ries were too painful to recall
I'll keep on loving you I'll be with you every night
Though you no longer care for me at all
After all my hope was gone of seeing you again
Now there's talk of a pardon for me
New evidence and confession of the guilty man
May free me but where will you be
It's too late for a pardon you don't want me anymore
They waited too long to set me free
I need to have your love again the way it was before
I won't get out until you pardon me

Damn, thought Joe, I'm on a roll this morning. Maybe I should turn in my shield and stay with the music business. He was dreaming again.

What happened later that morning was not a dream, but Joe wished it had been. A call from Ray Cauley left Joe feeling uncomfortable. "Joe, I tried to get in touch with you last night. Where were you?" Ray asked.

"I was right here but I was sleeping pretty heavy," said Joe. "Did you find Carla?"

Joe was anxious. When he had left the police station the previous afternoon Ray had assured him that he would go to the Jackson Boulevard apartment and check on Carla.

"There was no one at the place. Maybe Harry is covering something up," Ray offered.

"Did you check to see who lives there?" Joe was curious.

"Yea I checked with some of the other tenants but none of them could tell me anything. It's a pretty classy building and the neighbors tend to mind their own business. We're checking with the rental agent now, to see who the apartment was leased to last." Ray had finished.

Joe thanked Ray for keeping him informed then asked, "Could we take a ride over to Jackson Boulevard? I want to check a few things."

"Sure," said Ray. "I'll pick you up in say, thirty minutes."

As he waited for Ray a thought suddenly occurred to him. If Carla was taken to the apartment on Jackson Boulevard, then whoever lived there was acquainted with Susan. That is, assuming Harry was not lying. Joe's thoughts were interrupted by two quick blasts from the car horn.

When he left the room, Joe glanced sadly at his old friends that were sitting vigilantly on the table. Slamming the door, he rushed to the car where he was greeted by Ray.

Later, when they entered the apartment Joe quickly scanned the place. It was well furnished, small but efficient. He walked into the kitchen and methodically checked the cabinets then the refrigerator, noting that there was no food in either. Joe checked the apartment more thoroughly. Walking into the bathroom he noticed there was no toilet tissue to be found. This reinforced his suspicion that no one had lived here for some time. It was one thing not to have food in the house, but everyone had to have shit paper.

Joe saw it as he entered the room. It was lying on the floor at the foot of the bed. Only a small portion of the pale beige lounging gown was visible. "Ray!" Joe shouted. "Come here and take a look at this."

"What is it Joe?" Ray asked as he ran into the room. Joe pointed at the garment on the floor. "I was just about to remove that from Carla's lovely body when I was so rudely interrupted by Harry the other night. She's been here alright."

Ray picked up the garment and held the transparent gown at arm's length. The front of the gown was covered with dried blood.

"It appears like she's been wasted Joe."

"Let's hope not Ray." Joe spoke softly, barely audible. "She may be our only hope of solving four killings, if she's not number five."

Joe was in a trance on the way to the police station. He still wasn't sure what role Carla was playing in this drama. First, she was scared, then she would come up with a little information, then she would appear to be holding something back. Joe could only hope that he could find her, and she would be safe. He had some questions that only Carla could answer. And besides, he thought, there's a little matter of some unfinished business he had to discuss with her. He had not had the chance to finish the lyrics to her tune.

Joe was still daydreaming when Ray turned the ignition off. "Are you coming in Joe or are you going to sit here for a while?" Ray asked.

"Aha...No, I'm coming in."

Joe was becoming well known at the Nashville police station. "Hey, it's good to see you Joe,' said the sergeant at the desk. Then Ray was handed a written message. "This is the make on that Jackson Boulevard apartment Ray."

He read the message quickly and handed it to Joe. "You make anything out of this?" Ray asked. Joe read the message. The apartment had been leased to Robert Wesley five years ago. The lease was still current. He had heard the name but could not associate it with any of the present investigations. "No, the name doesn't ring a bell," said Joe, handing the paper back to Ray.

Joe stayed at the police station until 9:00 P.M. reading the case files on Jordon, Stoker, Deal and, searching for a possible connection, he read the Kenny Russell file once more. Although the DMV showed Carla's Volkswagen registered to Carla Love. Joe's instinct told him that Carla Love was formerly Carla Russell.

Carla and Susan both were prime suspects, Joe reflected on Ted Simpson's story. I can't let emotions enter into this investigation, he thought. Simpson's advice was the main reason Joe had waited so long to have the two women arrested. Just a few more loose ends. Joe had heeded Simpson's advice. He would not one day regret sending an innocent person up the creek for a crime they had not committed. Joe wanted solid evidence.

Entering his motel room at nearly 11:00 P.M., Joe closed the heavy metal door and leaned his head against its cool surface. He was mentally drained, but his thoughts would not slow down.

Then suddenly it hit him. It had been right under his nose and he could not grasp it. That's why he had lucked out, as Susan had put it. That's why he had not started production on his album that morning. The producer had had other things to do. Joe knew where he'd heard Robert Wesley's name.

Robert Wesley of MTM records. It was all taking shape now, but what was Robert Wesley's connection?

As Joe closed his eyes he thought, I'm going to dream about you tonight Julie. I'll be with you as soon as I can get to sleep. You could be with me too, if you were the dreaming kind.

Chapter Thirteen
Psycho Analysis

She was twenty-three when she had met Carlton. He was a brilliant, young electronics engineer major at Central University. She had high aspirations of one day obtaining her Masters in the field of Psychology. But as fate would have it, Susan Moore's college funds exhausted. It had happened to Susan all of her life, she would always lose-she'd been born a loser.

Growing up in Toledo, she had been a sickly child, and for that reason had not had many friends. The few close friends she did have she tried to possess. She held on to them for fear of losing them.

As the years went by Susan's health improved as did her list of friends. She became more popular at school, and her destitution for friends lessened considerably. She could not escape the obsession to possess. If you were Susan Moore's friend, she demanded exclusive rights to the friendship.

Susan was aware of her dominative nature. It had caused countless problems until she had learned to control it. She did not enjoy being the way she was but had learned to accept and live with it. Sessions with her psychoanalyst had helped her conceal her desire to possess, to a degree.

Susan Moore had secrets. Some things she could not even reveal to her analyst. Those awful things she had done, like giving her baby daughter away. Sure, it had been to relatives but that had made it even worse. Every time she had seen the child, she regretted it. Then she had met Carlton and after they were married, she had moved away, easing the turmoil of the situation. She had not seen her daughter since. For that matter she had totally avoided the relative to whom she had given the baby girl. The unwanted memories lay dormant for now but one day soon, sooner than she knew, her past would revive.

These early days when she and Carlton had first met, he had eyes only for her. This satisfied Susan's possessive nature. Everywhere Carlton went she was by his side. They were married one year after their first meeting. Soon after the wedding Carlton was no longer capable of providing Susan with the attention she craved. He was spending more and more time away from her.

Carlton's work kept him out of town for days. Susan, at home alone, had time to think. At night she would think lurid thoughts of her man, with other women. Gradually all the affection was gone, replaced by mistrust and resentment.

She now spent four hours each week with her analyst, who always gave her the attention she deserved. Susan needed more. She was not getting any younger but after ten years of marriage she was still attractive. Still she felt she was missing something from life. Nothing was exciting anymore.

One day during a session with her analyst it was suggested that she direct her energy towards a career. At thirty-four, she had started her publicity and promotions business in Nashville. Subconsciously she had chosen this business more for the attention it would provide her than for monetary gain.

She enjoyed the glamour of promoting the would-be stars. The ones who made it big were forever grateful to Susan. In her own twisted mind, she was their owner. She controlled their destiny. When she would see one of hers she would tell anyone who listened, "I own that singer," or "I own that actor." At last she was happy.

When Susan met Steve, he was broke and hungry. He had a guitar strapped to his back and a book of songs he had written, under his arm. He was a pitiful sight, hitch-hiking in the rain just north of Nashville. At first, she had passed the young man then she stopped her new, 1978 Cadillac, sliding on the wet pavement. She had backed the car to where Steve stood on the side of the road, lowered the electronically controlled window and asked, "Where you headed boy?"

"Nashville ma'am," was Steve's answer, as he got into the car. He was drenched.

"You a singer?" Susan was already plotting to own Steve.

"I do a little country." Steve was brief. Susan's beauty and apparent wealth cause him some embarrassment.

"I'll have to listen to you sometime. If I like what you do, I may be able to help you. I'm a promoter."

As things had turned out Susan had done more than listen to Steve. He was talented so she had no trouble booking him into some of Nashville's best clubs. His first performance was at the Western club. Steve had been grateful for everything Susan had done for him. She had only been in the promotion business for less than a year and Steve was her best promotion so far. To Susan he was a valued possession.

One night, Steve had come by the house on Magnolia. It was late and Susan and Carlton were having one of their frequent arguments. This was a common practice in the Jordon household. By this time their marriage had deteriorated to the point of no repair. While Steve was there Carlton struck Susan in the face with his fist. Steve had protected her from serious injury by stopping Carlton. Susan had been sitting on the floor, face swelling from the blow, lips bleeding, when Carlton left the house in a rage. He never returned.

Later that evening Steve made an appearance at a party in downtown Nashville. He was high on drugs and carrying a gun. Steve had muttered something about killing some asshole. The very next morning Carlton was found, his lifeless body slumped over the steering wheel of his car. There were two bullet holes in his head.

When Steve showed up at the recording studio his bass player was already there. He watched as Steve removed the backing from the Peavy amplifier and place something inside. When the bass player heard the news of Carlton's death, he suspected Steve had murdered Carlton. The bass player was very observant and had noticed Steve and Susan had become very attached these last few months.

She and Steve were together frequently until Susan hired Carla. When he started to pay more attention to Carla. She knew she had lost him to her younger, more beautiful secretary.

Mr. Wesley noticed Susan's reaction to Steve rejecting her. He had secretly admired Susan for a long time but had not approached her while Carlton had been living. With Carlton gone she would be free, that's what Wesley had thought. Then Steve had put a stop to any plan he'd had of pursuing an affair with Susan.

Suddenly Steve had been killed while doing a show in Dallas. It was all so mysterious. She had been shocked when the news of Steve's sudden death was relayed to her. Wesley had made it a point to be there to comfort her, to help her through that mournful period of her life.

It was about a month later that Wesley suggested she promote another singer. "The boy needs a break, and you should do something to occupy your time," he had suggested. The boy was Denny Deal. Wesley had spoken so highly of him that she had decided to give him a chance, after all he had been Steve's bass player. Denny didn't sing bad, but he didn't have the talent Steve had been blessed with. The next few weeks Susan devoted most of her time to making Denny Deal a star.

Before long Susan was unintentionally becoming romantically involved with Denny. Wesley was extremely upset over this foul turn of events. He had not expected this to happen. He had seen them together, the way they behaved, and knew that it was only a matter of time before he would lose Susan again.

Since Carlton's death Susan had not been treated rough by any man. But here she was in a motel room with a strange man, whose name she did not know. He was shouting at her. She was afraid and in a strange sort of way the fear was exciting. This man could be the answer to her lifelong problem that so many psychoanalysts had failed to help her with. This man had scared her. She knew instantly that she could never own a man like this. Susan accepted this fact and decided to like him anyway.

All this killing going on around her had Susan so emotionally upset that she had doubled her appointments with her analyst. She had been with Denny at his apartment moments before he had been killed. Susan was ready for a nervous breakdown.

As if she did not have enough problems, Wesley had started behaving strange. Just two days ago he had given her an attaché case and an envelope and instructed her to hold them until Harry Fellman came by for them. Unwittingly Susan did as Wesley had instructed. She had given Harry the envelope one evening then the attaché case the following morning.

And now her faithful secretary Carla had deserted her. Right when she needed her most. Carla had not showed up at work for two days now. Susan's head was about to explode from all the pressure as she entered the professional building. Her analyst's office was on the third floor. She always felt relieved after her visits here, but Susan Jordon knew she needed more than she could ever get from a psychoanalyst.

Chapter Fourteen
The Power of Suggestion

Some people will do anything with a little prompting, thought Robert Wesley. He was at the recording studio to hear the new album Steve was recording. All during the rehearsals he noticed that Steve had acted eccentric, screaming at Denny for the most insignificant things. Wesley knew that Denny despised Steve. It was obvious from the way he glared at him.

After the rehearsals were completed the group broke for lunch. Denny remained behind so Wesley decided to chat with him. "You know son, if someone talked to me like that, I'd kill the son-of-a-bitch. Who does he think he is to treat you like that?"

Wesley knew the animosity Denny already felt towards Steve. He thought, 'this would be an excellent chance for me to have Steve done away with and I would never be suspected of anything.'

Robert Wesley spent weeks programming Denny Deal, dropping seemingly innocent suggestions at just the appropriate moment. Usually when he knew that Steve had just made Denny mad, Wesley spent hours talking to Denny. Finally, Denny could take it no longer. The power of suggestion, that's what drove him to remove the backing from the amplifier. Denny's hands were shaking as he reached inside and removed the gun.

That night when Steve's tour bus left for Dallas the bass player was not aboard. Denny had walked out earlier that day. He told Steve that he could not take the pressures of the road anymore. The following evening at the Silver Horse café two shots rang out. Steve lay dead on the stage with two bullet holes in his head.

Denny wasted no time in Dallas, he caught a bus and was back in Nashville early the next morning. He went directly to the recording studio to retrieve his equipment, Robert

Wesley was already there, consoling Susan. She had just heard the news about Steve.

Denny walked into the recording studio, followed closely by Wesley. When they were alone Wesley said, "You did it, by god you finally did it. You killed the son-of-a-bitch. I was beginning to think you didn't have the balls."

His hands shook as Denny returned the gun to its hiding place then replaced the backing on the amplifier. As Wesley watched he said, "Boy don't shake so hard, nobody knows but you and me. I ain't telling, are you?"

Denny tried to smile but his lips were dry and cracking it hurt something awful to even talk. "Thanks Mr. Wesley," Denny said, wincing at the pain his lips caused.

Wesley then told Denny to disappear for a while until things blew over. "Check back with me in about a month I'll have a job for you. You're a good boy Denny."

Everything went according to Wesley's plan; Susan had accepted his consoling and had even started to return some of the affection he had shown for her then Denny came back. Wesley, a man of his word, arranged for Denny a job as he had promised he would. That promise would have been broken had Robert Wesley known he stood a chance of losing Susan again.

Wesley followed Susan as she went to the apartment on West 31st Street and angrily waited outside for a few minutes. There was only one way he could have her to himself, he thought. Wesley returned to the recording studio, removed the gun from the amplifier where he'd seen Denny put it over a year ago, then drove back to Denny's apartment.

Susan's car was still in the parking lot which made him furious. I'll kill them both, he thought, as he gripped the handle of the .38 and started up the stairs to the second floor. He opened the door to enter the corridor then stopped abruptly. Susan was standing there, nose buried in her purse searching for something. Probably looking for her car keys, he thought.

Quietly Wesley darted into the maid's cleaning closet, Susan was not aware of his presence.

Susan found whatever she had been looking for and walked down the corridor, past the closet where Wesley was hiding and out of the building. When he could no longer hear her footsteps, Wesley left the cramped room and walked to Denny's apartment, 2C.

He stood outside for a moment, thinking, the son-of-a-bitch would still be in bed. He let himself into the apartment. Denny was in the bedroom, not in bed but standing near the window, he did not hear Wesley enter the room. When he realized that someone was in the room it was too late to react. Denny turned and looked straight at Wesley then the last thing he saw was the barrel of the .38 caliber pistol.

Two shots were fired, ironically both bullets struck Denny in the head. As he fell lifelessly to the carpeted floor the Pentax 35mm camera fell from the dead man's hand. Wesley picked the camera up from the floor, took it to the dark room, then hurriedly left the apartment.

He had taken no more than two steps into the corridor when he was greeted by Carla, "Hi Mr. Wesley!" she said. Oh shit, he thought, what's she doing here? Carla's arms were filled with groceries as she passed him in the hallway. Wesley hoped she was not going to Denny's apartment. He spoke to her and quickly ran from the building.

Wesley drove back to Magnolia and returned the gun to its hiding place. The .38 caliber revolver had only been removed twice since Steve had placed it there originally. Wesley was starting to worry now; he should have never left that girl alive. She'd know that he killed Denny which meant that he had to keep her silent somehow.

Two days later he was at Hogan's bar, Harry, a local drunk was, as usual, talking about the vacation that he never had. Harry could use some money and Wesley was sure Harry would be an easy victim to the power of suggestion. Robert Wesley had a long talk with Harry. "I suggest you take that vacation Harry." He started. "There's a lady I know that needs a little favor done if you're interested, I'm sure she would be very generous."

"What would I have to do?" Harry asked, interested.

"Just follow a few simple directions from a typewritten card," Wesley answered, designing a scheme as the conversation progressed. "Here's my card, give me a call when you've made your decision." Wesley was calm as he got up from the table. "I suggest you take that vacation Harry." Saluting Harry, Wesley left the bar.

Just after noon Harry called the number from the card Wesley had given him. He had been drinking heavily since their conversation at Hogan's. "This is Harry, what do I have to do?"

Wesley told him to go to 612 Magnolia and Susan would give him an envelope containing the instructions. He was to read and comply with the instructions. The envelope would also contain $500.00 advance money. After he had carried out the instructions Harry would return to Susan's the next morning for the rest of his pay. "Simple Harry, you will be on that jet tomorrow, on your way to Europe." Wesley told the drunken Harry.

Harry followed Wesley's instructions; he went to the house on Magnolia, Susan gave him the envelope and he left. When he was back inside his Buick, he quickly tore open the envelope and removed the five crisp one-hundred-dollar bills and a 3X5 inch card. The simple typewritten instructions were;

Go to 35 Washington Avenue, Kill Carla Love

and take her body to 215 Jackson Boulevard.

Don't forget Harry, $10,000.00 is yours in the morning…

Harry thought he should not go through with this but ten grand was a lot of money. Hell, if he had to, he could stay out of the country for a long time with that kind of money. Against his better judgement he went to the house on Washington avenue, forced his way in, and waited for Carla to come home.

When he heard the car pull into the driveway, he looked through the drapes and saw them. A man was with her, he had expected Carla to be alone. Harry became frightened and quickly hid in the closet by the entrance door. He wanted only to escape from the house somehow, but it was too late for that now they were coming in the front door at that very moment.

Later, as Carla and Joe sat on the sofa necking Harry suddenly had a burst of courage or fear. He quietly slipped from the closet and grabbed the bottle of Jack Daniel's from the table behind Joe. Carla saw Harry and screamed. The frightened man struck Joe on the back of the head dropping the bottle, unbroken, behind the sofa.

Joe slumped forward, his head buried in Carla's lap, unconscious. Carla continued to scream as Harry struck her several times. Carla's screams finally stopped, she was bleeding and unconscious when Harry ceased beating her. He then threw her over his shoulder, walked out of the house and dumped her body in the back seat of his Buick.

As instructed Harry took Carla to 215 Jackson Boulevard where he placed her on the bed. Harry Fellman was physically and mentally drained. All would have gone well except for the fact Carla was not dead.

Wesley went to the apartment the next morning expecting to find Carla's dead body. At first, he too thought she was dead, there was dried blood all over her. He moved closer to the beaten woman and could see her breast rise and fall as she breathed.

He thought quickly, desperate now he had to get her out of this apartment. He shook Carla until she opened her eyes. She became hysterical when she saw Wesley.

"Calm down," he said, "No one is going to hurt you."

Several minutes later Wesley had succeeded in calming Carla. Somehow, he convinced her that he had not killed

Denny Deal. He told her to get cleaned up and as she showered, Wesley laid some clothes on the bed for her.

After her shower Carla felt some better but was still hurting all over. She and Wesley were now in his car somewhere in Nashville. They had not been in the car long when Wesley parked in front of 17 New Jersey street. He got out of the car and Carla followed. As they entered the building he said, "Carla this is my office and I want you to stay here until I come back for you. Don't answer the phone or let anyone in. You will be safe here until I can find out who did this to you."

Wesley needed time to think, he knew he could not let Carla live but he was not capable of killing the girl himself. Since he had shot Denny, he had been a bundle of nerves. He was unable to concentrate. Harry the son-of-a-bitch, was already out of the country by now. Wesley tried Harry's phone number again, but the phone just kept ringing. He angrily slammed the phone back on its cradle. Harry had pulled a quick one, took the money and left the job unfinished. Fuck it, so much for the power of suggestion, he thought.

Chapter Fifteen
Smith and Wesson

When Smith and Wesson designed the .38 caliber revolver, they did not design it for the purpose of murder. Numerous murders have been committed with this type of weapon since then. Joe was interested in only one weapon at the present time-the .38 caliber Smith & Wesson he had accidentally discovered when he had moved the amplifier at 612 Magnolia. It was time to get that weapon to ballistics for some tests.

Ray and Joe went to the legal building and rode the elevator to the eighth floor. Judge Bates greeted them both with a broad smile, he had known Ray for a long time. Joe told Judge Bates how he had discovered the weapon. When he finished, leaving some of the details out-Judge Bates said, "Since you were authorized to be at the recording studio, and it was an unofficial discovery, I think we can use your information to give Ray the probable cause he is required to have for a legal search. I'm satisfied that a crime has been committed and that the weapon you have described could possibly have been used to commit the crime or crimes."

Judge Bates signed the search warrant and handed it to Ray. Both detectives thanked the kind Judge and left his office. Once they were safely in the elevator Joe said, "Do you think I should have told the good judge the weapon was discovered during the commission of a burglary?" Both men laughed.

The house at 612 Magnolia was unoccupied when the unmarked police car pulled into the driveway and parked. Ray and Joe got out of the car and walked to the front door. Ray touched the button to ring the doorbell. After several rings there was still no answer, they entered the house anyway since the door was not locked. As soon as they were inside Joe led the way to the recording studio. He wasted no time in removing the backing from the Peavy amplifier.

Joe sighed in relief; the Smith & Wesson was still there. Ray took the weapon, handling it carefully to preserve any fingerprints that may be on the gun. He placed the gun in a plastic evidence bag and marked the bag with his initials, time, date and the location where the weapon had been found. This procedure had become routine for Ray. They had found the object of their search so, legally they could search no further. They left Susan's with the most valuable piece of real evidence they had found, if the tests were positive, if not they would be no closer to solving the murders than they had been a week ago.

It was a short ride back to the crime lab where they gave the weapon to Igor. "I'll get right on these tests gentlemen. I should know the results in three or four hours you are welcome to stay and observe if you'd like," Igor invited.

"No, we have some things to do, just call the station when you get the results please," Joe quickly declined Igor's invitation, not in the mood for another lecture on forensic science.

Joe planned his next move, if the weapon tested positive it was the murder weapon and would confirm his suspicion. He could confront Susan with the evidence. She was involved in murder; Joe was sure of it. He thought of Ted Simpson's advice.

They were back in the car, Ray wheeling in and out of traffic, He had absolutely no reason to be driving so recklessly. "Why are you driving like a mad man?" Joe asked.

"This is the only way I know how to drive," Ray replied, "That's why I joined the department-I like to drive fast." They laughed as Ray swerved to the right to miss an oncoming car and nearly struck a parked one.

As they passed by Washington street Joe made the mistake of asking Ray to drive by Carla's. Ray nodded and quickly turned the wheel to the right. Joe had to grab the door to prevent sliding into the crazy driver. "Remind me never to ride with you again."

"It beats the hell out of yellow cab, right?"

Carla's Volkswagen was still parked in the driveway. Inside the house everything appeared to be just the way it had been when Joe was last there. Joe saw the bottle of Jack Daniel's lying on the floor behind the sofa, so that's what Harry had hit him with. "Jack Daniel's is out to get me one way or another," he told Ray, as he retrieved the bottle.

Joe searched the house again for any clue he may have missed the night of the abduction, he had been groggy from the blow on his head then and possibly could have missed something. In the bedroom while shuffling through a drawer filled with old cards and letters, he found one letter that aroused his interest. It was addressed to Carla Russell, he opened the envelope and read the brief note;

You are free now. What are friends for?

The note was unsigned, another reason Joe thought it strange, but it meant nothing to him. The name on the envelope however meant a great deal, it proved Joe's theory that Carla Love was Carla Russell. The same Carla Russell that had been questioned in the Kenny Russell homicide.

Joe returned everything back to the way it had been before he started his search then walked into the other room where Ray was searching. "Carla Love used to be Carla Russell, Ray."

"You mean the one from the OD case you were reading?"

"Exactly," Joe sounded distant. He had suspected it since the day he had read the Russell homicide file in the records cemetery. Now he had ammunition to use against Carla if she had not already become the target for a very different kind of ammunition. "Let's go Ray, there ain't shit that's going to help us here."

As they got into the unmarked police car Ray asked, "Can I drop you somewhere?"

"Yea, drop me by Susan's."

This time Susan's Cadillac was there, parked in the driveway. Good, she's home, Joe thought. As he walked into the house unannounced, he shouted Susan's name.

"I'm back here!"

Joe walked in the direction of the voice which led him to one of the guest rooms. "Oh, here you are," Joe said, finding Susan. "Where is Carla?" Joe wanted to see what her reaction would be.

"She hasn't been to work for three days now. I don't know what has happened to her. I've called her house several times but get no answer. Frankly Joe, I'm worried about her."

When Joe sprung the next question on Susan, he still could not detect any unusual expression, nor did her behavior change. "Susan do you own a gun?"

"Why sure but I don't use it, I haven't seen it for over six years. Why Joe?"

"Some people have been following me and I was going to borrow it for protection." Joe lied, not ready to reveal his true motive for the questioning.

"Let's see where did Carlton put that gun? He used to keep it in the table by our bed, but I was afraid for it to stay there. We didn't get along very well near the end and I was afraid he might come in drunk one night and shoot me," Susan explained.

"It's really important, do you think you could find it?"

"We'll look for it," she said, seemingly not one bit surprised by Joe's mention of the gun.

The next hour was spent searching the house for the weapon. Susan appeared genuine in her efforts to find it. Joe's plan was in effect but so far it was proving nothing. "Maybe someone stole it," Susan finally suggested.

"What kind of gun was it? Could you describe it? Was it an automatic or revolver?" Joe fired questions at her deliberately so she would not be allowed the chance to fabricate a story, any answers she gave would more than likely be true.

"What's the difference? I just know it was a gun."

"Did you still have the sales receipt for the gun? If it was stolen it should be reported," Joe told her.

"That, I can probably find, Carlton always kept his receipts."

The searching started all over again. If murder had not been the issue at the base of the inquiries Joe would have thought the scene comical. All of his efforts seemed to be wasted on this woman. Susan had done it again; she had thrown him yet another curve. Joe still could not be one hundred percent sure she had committed the murders, but she had to be involved in some way. The mystery was, how?

Half an hour later Susan found the receipt. "This must be it," she handed Joe a piece of paper. "Does it say what kind of gun it was Joe?"

"Yes Susan, it's a revolver, Smith & Wesson," he said as he copied down the serial number. "Smith & Wesson," Joe repeated.

Chapter Sixteen
Wanted Man in Tennessee

When Ray and Joe met at the station the next morning, they decided to interrogate Harry again. It had been three days since his arrest, maybe his story had changed slightly. They had the jailer bring Harry to the interrogation room.

"Look Harry, is there anything else you can tell us?" Ray started.

"I've told you everything already," Harry said nervously.

"Bullshit!" Joe shouted, slapping the table with his open hand. "You're lying your ass off." Joe continued to shout at Harry. "We haven't found Carla yet, but we did find her blood-soaked gown. What do you know about that Harry?" Joe was angry or appeared to be.

Harry grasped his head in both his hands and exclaimed, "I didn't mean to hurt her, but she kept screaming, I lost my head, I guess! I kept beating her until the screaming stopped!" Harry was crying again.

"Be straight now Harry, are you and Susan the only two involved in the abduction of Carla?" Joe had stopped shouting and was now almost sympathetic.

Harry was calming down some himself but still sniffled as he answered Joe. "As far as I know I was doing it for Susan. There's this guy named Wesley that approached me with the suggestion that same morning at Hogan's bar. He's the one who arranged for me to contact Susan." Harry Fellman told the detectives about his conversation with Robert Wesley. "Wesley gave me his business card and told me to contact him if I was interested." Harry completed his confession, stopping several times to dry his eyes.

Two hours after his confession Harry was back in his cell, but he could not stop shaking. He thought, what if that girl is dead? I'll never get out of jail. Hell, they could even execute me, he started to cry again. Harry Fellman was paying for his one and only crime.

Ray went to the property room and asked the custodian to check Harry's belongings. "Just check his wallet for a business card of Mister Wesley."

"Right," the custodian answered, as he slowly moved from his chair to locate Fellman's things. The process was much too slow for the impatient Ray but somehow, he held on for the fifteen minutes it took the custodian to find what he'd asked for.

"This must be what you're looking for," he said as he placed the business card on the counter for Ray to copy. Ray was silent as he wrote;

> Robert Wesley MTM Records
>
> 17 New Jersey Street
>
> Nashville, TN
>
> Telephone 446-5667

Ray returned to the interrogation room and gave Joe the information from Wesley's card. Joe, who had been leaning in a tilted chair, nearly lost his balance when he read-17 New Jersey-the goddamned dream. He decided against saying anything to Ray, who already thought Joe was weird but to satisfy his own mind he thought they should check the address. "We should give Wesley a call," said Joe.

"Hell, let's just drive over, there's no sense giving him a warning." Ray smiled.

"Only if I do the driving. If I ride with you, I'll be back on the sauce in no time." Joe held out his hand for the car keys. The good-natured Ray laughed and handed them over.

Carla was still groggy from the beating, her head ached and throbbed with the slightest movement. Wesley had promised her that it would be safe to go home any day now, she was uncomfortable here, but it was better than going home and taking a chance on being killed. She heard someone enter the outer office, thinking it may be her attacker she quickly opened the window and climbed onto the fire escape, she would be safe there temporarily.

Joe and Ray searched the offices thoroughly but to no avail. "Nothing here," Ray said. So much for a damned dream, thought Joe, discouraged that his dream had meant nothing. They searched through the desk drawers looking for anything which would connect Wesley further with Carla's abduction. Harry's story had to be verified.

As they were about to leave Joe happened to glance into a waste basket behind the desk. There were several 3X5 inch, typewritten cards lying on top of some other papers. Joe retrieved one and read it-Go to 37-, then another-Go to 35 Washer- the cards interested Joe, so he took them with him when he and Ray left the office.

In the car Ray asked, "What now Joe?"

"It's time to make some arrests Ray." Joe reflected on Ted Simpson's philosophy once again, shit Ted, he thought, how sure do I have to be? Then, "We'll drive by Judge Bates office he already knows the case so maybe we can get warrants for the arrests of Susan and Wesley," said Joe as he dropped the gearshift of the unmarked police car into DRIVE.

When they arrived at Judge Bates' office he was on the bench, but they did not have to wait long. Court recessed for lunch then the good judge entered his chambers to find Ray and Joe waiting for him. Judge Bates said he would be happy to help them, Ray had not embarrassed him previously with improper warrant requests, so he had no reason to expect this request to be illegitimate.

The process of getting an arrest warrant was usually time consuming, requiring twenty to thirty good lies but since Judge Bates had known Ray the whole process took less than an hour.

They wasted the rest of the afternoon driving all over Nashville searching for Susan and Wesley. All their efforts were dead ends, the suspects were not to be found. Composite pictures of both suspects were sketched by a police artist at Joe's request. All the Nashville area television stations aired the sketches on the six o'clock news broadcast still the suspects were not located.

Watching the news broadcast at his motel room Joe thought, Susan will not be difficult to locate, she craved attention too much to hide out for very long but Wesley, that's another matter. Tonight, Robert Wesley was a wanted man in Tennessee.

His career in the music industry had ended. The two people who could have helped him most were about to be arrested and Joe would be responsible for their arrests. He had a feeling of gratification knowing the murders were nearly solved but on the other hand he was somber. Dismal because he had not been able to find Carla, dejected for now he may never know how far he could have gone in the music industry. Woefully he wrote;

Wanted Man in Tennessee

Every time I see the muddy Mississippi
I think about old times in Tennessee
I remember all the times I left her
All the times she's come back to me
After all the bad ways I've done her
I don't know how she could still love me
Every time I let my mind wander
I think about old times in Tennessee
If it was a crime to be foolish
If it was a crime to set her free
If it was a crime to break her heart and make her cry
I'd be a wanted man in Tennessee
If it hadn't been for all the times I left her
If I'd listened when she begged me not to leave
If I would have shown her just a little love
I'd be a wanted man in Tennessee

The next morning Joe got a taxi to take him to Susan's. When he arrived, her Cadillac was not in the drive, but Joe got out of the taxi anyway. He wanted to be there when Susan came home to let her know how he felt about her. He had not liked Susan at first but since he had learned to deal with her personality and ego mania, she wasn't so bad. Joe especially admired her brusque style of letting people know what she wanted. If only she were not involved in murder.

When the telephone rang Joe instinctively jumped up to answer it then heard the beep as the answering machine was activated. He turned the volume up so he could hear who was calling.

"Susan, this is Bob. I'll be going to my office for a while then I have to get away from Nashville for a few days, the stress is getting to me, we could take my private plane and just fly away somewhere together. Think about it." Bob hung up and the recorder whirred as it saved the message.

Joe immediately contacted Ray and told him to get over to Susan's right away. It was not necessary to tell Ray to hurry Joe assumed he would anyway.

Ray arrived fifteen minutes later as Joe had expected. The drive from the police station to Susan's would have taken anyone thirty minutes-anyone except Ray Cauley. Joe played back the taped message for Ray who said, "Maybe, we can get him before he leaves his office."

"If you'll hurry, we can catch him before he gets out of his car," said Joe, momentarily forgetting about Ray's reckless driving.

When they pulled into the parking lot at 17 New Jersey Joe recognized the tall thin man immediately. Before the detectives arrested Robert Wesley, Joe thought about the song he had just written and laughed.

> If it was a crime to be foolish
> If it was a crime to set you free
> If it was a crime to break your heart and make you cry
> I'd be a wanted man in Tennessee

Chapter Seventeen
Six Bullets One Gun

Igor was thorough as he conducted test after test. He wanted to be positive the weapon was the same one that had fired all of the bullet fragments. He made several comparisons using the peripheral photographs from each of the homicide reports. The Stoker and Deal specimens were positive, no question about those two, however, Igor had some difficulties with the Jordon specimen. After several comparisons he was able to satisfy his own mind, the Jordon specimen was also positive. There was no doubt in Igor's scientific mind that the suspected murder weapon had fired all six bullets.

It was late when Igor tried to reach Joe and Ray at the police station, they had already left for the day, so he left a message with the clerk on duty. "Tell them I said sorry for the delay, but science cannot be rushed. The weapon they brought in is positively the one used in all three homicide cases. I'll send them a written report of my findings." Igor was mechanical as he gave the clerk the oral report.

Just before hanging up Igor said, "Oh yea, also tell them the only latent prints that could be lifted from the gun were smudged but they appear to be those of a man. Goodbye."

He would soon have the Stoker homicide all wrapped up if they could only find Susan. Wesley was already in jail, but he was a hard case. He had requested counsel and would not say a word. The unfortunate thing was that there was not a lot they could hold him on. If something didn't break soon Wesley would have to be released on bail. He was wealthy enough to leave the country and Joe could not let that happen. Wesley surely had left some evidence somewhere; Joe would just have to dig until he found it.

After lunch Joe asked Ray to drive them over to Stir Publishing company. They found the address in the yellow pages and were on their way. As usual Ray had a four-hundred-pound foot and rested it all on the accelerator.

"How many cars do you go through for the department in a year?" Joe asked, holding on to his door.

"I ain't wrecked one yet," said Ray, then he added, "that was my fault." Both men laughed.

The entire third floor of the building was occupied by Stir Publishing Company. At the receptionist's desk Joe asked, "Is this where I go to find Mr. Thompson?"

"Mr. Thompson is in a meeting right now sir and is not taking any calls. Would you care to make an appointment for later?"

She was polite but it was urgent Joe must see Thompson and right now. "Show the lady your shield Ray?"

"Which office did you say was Mr. Thompson's?" Ray asked, showing the receptionist his police shield.

"It's the fourth one on the left," she said, surrendering as she pushed the intercom button to warn Thompson of the intruders.

"What can I do for you gentlemen?" Asked Mr. Thompson.

"I met you a few days ago at 612 Magnolia, Susan Jordon introduced us."

"Oh, that's right, Joe Rudolf the singer, right?"

"Ruddy," Joe corrected Thompson.

"Did Wesley contact you yet Ruddy?"

"I have to tell you Mr. Thompson, I'm not really a singer, I'm a police officer here on assignment from Dallas."

"You could have fooled me son, you sounded like a singer when I heard you at the recording studio." Thompson smiled then said, "I liked the songs you wrote fact is I told Wesley I'd be glad to publish your work."

"Thanks for the compliment but right now sir we're trying to solve an abduction case or possibly a murder. I'm afraid Mr. Wesley is a prime suspect," Joe told the elderly music publisher.

"I see. But how can I help?" Thompson asked, sitting down at the enormous oak desk.

"I assume you've known Robert Wesley for a long time, am I correct?" Joe guessed.

"About ten years at least. He's a good man."

"Do you know anything about his private life with Susan Jordon?" Joe was fishing now.

"He lost his wife back in '77 they had been really close. Then he met Susan at a public release of a record which he had produced. This was shortly after his wife died. Wesley talked about Susan quite a lot." Thompson was silent for a moment, then he resumed talking. "Then Susan's husband died or was killed or whatever. Anyway, Robert started seeing her frequently for about a month, that's when the boy Susan was promoting came into the picture," Mr. Thompson recalled.

"Which boy is that?" Joe asked quickly.

"Steve something, I'm terrible with names."

"Steve Stoker?" Joe prompted.

"That's the one. Susan started spending all her time with that Steve character and Robert was very upset. A few months later Steve was killed. It was big news here in Nashville, him a country singer and all. Robert wasted no time in getting things patched up between himself and Susan. Hell, he even found her a new singer to promote-Denny somebody." Thompson hardly took time for a deep breath before he started again. "Robert was insanely obsessed with Susan."

"You're saying Robert Wesley was in love with Susan Jordon?" Ray got into the conversation.

"It was obvious," replied Thompson, "All he did was talk about her. He encouraged me and a few others to help her with her promotions, that's why I was there the day I met you Buddy."

"Ruddy," Joe corrected again.

"What? Oh yea, Ruddy. Well anyway right after Susan got this Denny character started good, Robert started to complain about her not having time for him anymore. It was the same thing all over again, he stopped seeing Susan only this time I thought it was over between them, then this past week or two he's done nothing but talk about her." Mr. Thompson had finished.

"Have you seen him recently?" Joe asked.

"A day or so ago he said he was going to fly to the Bahamas with Susan, that was the last time I saw him.

"Have you noticed anything strange about him the last few days?" Joe continued to question.

"Robert Wesley is always strange but his obsession with Susan Jordon is sickening. With his money he could have any woman but instead he lets Susan drive him crazy."

"Thanks for your time sir, I think you may have answered some key questions. At least you have cleared some things up for me." Joe was grateful.

As Joe and Ray started to leave the office Mr. Thompson said, "Joe if you ever need a publisher don't hesitate to call me. I'm always open for fresh material."

"Thanks sir, I'll keep that in mind." Joe waved and closed the door on his way out.

Ray waved at the receptionist as he passed her, she gave them an unfriendly snarl. As soon as they were in the car Joe spoke first, "Are you thinking what I'm thinking?"

"Robert Wesley's at the bottom of this mess of worms?" Ray asked.

"Exactly! We've got to find Carla before it's too late. The way I've got it figured she knew too much, that's why someone, probably Wesley, had to remove her from the picture. This whole damned thing is starting to make no sense at all now. But there's one thing that's really got me confused Ray."

"What's that?" Ray tried to make it through the caution light unsuccessfully, he ran the red light.

"Three murders, six bullets, and one gun," said Joe, resting his head against the seat back.

Chapter Eighteen
A Slew of Clues

Murdered or suspected murdered:

1. *Carlton Jordon*

2. *Kenny Russell*

3. *Steve Cranston (alias Steve Stoker)*

4. *Denny Deal*

5. *Carla Love (Russell)?*

Joe outlined the events on the chalk board. It reminded Ray of his high school coach laying out a game plan.

"Now, we have to add everything we have so far, put all the clues together. A homicide is like a painting-each clue is a part of that painting, a mere brushstroke. If you take one brushstroke by itself it doesn't mean much but put several together on canvas, add just a little talent and some form of art develops. So, Ray, let's put our heads together and draw a picture. When we finish, we should be able to recognize the characters."

Joe turned back to the chalk board and continued to write;

Suspects:

1. *Susan Jordon*

2. *Denny Deal*

3. *Carla Love (Russell)*

4. *Robert Wesley*

5. *Harry Fellman*

Abduction/Kidnapping
      Victim   *Suspects*

  Carla Love (Russell)   *1. Robert Wesley*

                             2. Susan Jordon

                             3. Harry Fellman

Joe stopped writing and turned to face Ray once again. "These are the characters Ray do you have anyone to add to the lists?"

"That about covers them."

Joe moved to the other side of the chalk board and started a new list;

Clues/Evidence

1. *Six bullet fragments removed from the scene (either from the victim or the crime scenes)*

2. *One .38 caliber Smith & Wesson revolver*

3. *All characters are connected with the music industry (not sure about Kenny Russell)*

4. *Note found on Toyota (Who wrote it?)*

5. *Carla's bloody gown*

6. *Typewritten 3x5 cards*

7. *Drug connection (Kenny Russell's overdose and Steve Stoker's habit)*

8. *Harry's loose tongue at Hogan's bar*

9. *Susan's reaction to Harry's presence at the bar*

10. *The photograph of the purse*

11. *The message Wesley left on the answering machine*

12. *The phone call Susan allegedly received from Denny*

13. *The receipt for the gun*

14. *Carla's trip to Kentucky with Steve*

15. *Denny's eagerness to volunteer information*

16. *Susan's possessiveness and jealousy*

17. *The yellow skirt*

18. *Susan's mention of her husband's death*

19. *Carla's reluctance to talk when Wesley had been at Susan's*

20. *Gary Turner's statement (Susan's threat to kill Steve)*

21. *Harry at Susan's after the kidnapping*

22. *Carla's nervousness the morning after Denny's death*

23. *The lens cover*

24. *Wesley leased the apartment at 215 Jackson*

25. *Finding the Russell case accidentally*

26. *DMV check of Carla's VW*

27. *Harry's confession*

Joe stopped writing when he had completely covered the chalk board. He laughed then turned to Ray and said, "From looking at this mess it would appear they all killed each other." Joe didn't know how close he had come to the truth.

When they walked out of the detective squad room the familiar desk sergeant passed them in the hallway. "Say, did you guys get the message from the crime lab? They found some prints on that gun you took in. It was the murder weapon according to the lab. They said they would send a report."

Joe thought quickly then said. "Has Wesley been released yet?"

"No, but if we don't charge him, he'll have to be cut loose in four hours," said the sergeant.

"Could you get me his fingerprint card?" Joe requested.

The sergeant nodded and walked into the records and administration office. A few minutes later he returned with two fingerprint cards, containing Wesley's prints. Joe took the cards and said, "Thanks Sarge," then turning to Ray, "Crime lab Ray, you drive, I'm in a hurry!"

Ray wheeled the undercover vehicle out of the police parking lot, colliding with the curb as he turned right. Joe talked to take his mind off Ray's driving. "If these prints match those lifted from the gun Wesley won't make bail today," Joe slapped the cards against the seat.

It was Igor's day off. Another lab technician said he would be glad to help. Ray and Joe waited in the staff lounge, too excited to sit they paced the floor for over an hour. When the lab technician entered the lounge and handed Joe a typewritten lab report of the fingerprint comparisons, he was afraid to look but forced himself to.

"What's the verdict Joe?" Ray, as usual, was impatient.

"We've got our man!" Joe gave a yell. "We can add Wesley's fingerprints to our list of clues," Joe said, smiling.

Captain Miller had been glad to hear from Joe the last time he'd called. The progress he'd reported had kept Chief Reynolds off Miller's back for three whole days. "Harman," Miller said, "Has Joe called this morning?"

Harmon, the black detective answered using Southern Black colloquialism, "No, but I be right here if he call boss."

"Don't let him hang up, I have to talk to him."

"You got it boss."

About noon the telephone rang at the detective bureau of the Dallas PD. Harmon, who had been sleeping with his head on the desk woke up when he heard Miller's voice boom through the office. "Answer the goddamned phone Harmon!" He did not know which had woke him, the phone ringing or Captain Miller's shouting. He picked up the receiver, "Dallas PD, Detective Harmon, may I help you?"

"Hey Chuck, let me talk to the Captain," said Joe.

"Miller here, how's it going?' Miller boomed into the phone he had been on the extension.

"Captain I should have this thing wrapped up soon. I have made two arrests and have a warrant for one more. There could be others but I'm not sure about that yet. Our big break came with the discovery of the murder weapon. The crime lab has completed the comparison tests, it seems the weapon that killed Stoker is the same one used for the two murders here in Nashville." Joe explained the details.

"Sounds like you've been busy, good work Joe." Miller was pleased.

"Thanks Captain, I'll know more after we make the other arrest. Not much else to say this time." Joe finished his report.

After the phone call Joe suddenly became hungry. He had not been eating or drinking much lately and had started to trim down. He ate a light supper at the motel restaurant then returned to his room.

Joe's list of clues was still incomplete. He had not listed the dreams. The nightmare that had taken place in the dark alley in Germany had been a clue to the drug involvement. The football jersey bearing the number 17 had also been significant but Joe was still uncertain about that. One reason he had not listed them was he did not want Ray to know that he took his dreams seriously. Something that would later prove to be a clue Joe had held in his hands. He had stared at it but to him it had not been significant. He had not included it in his slew of clues.

Chapter Nineteen
The Arrests

Crime, like any other event in this universe, must follow a chronological order of occurrence. First comes the motive or the reason the crime was committed, then the crime. In most cases the offender leaves behind some clue. The problem arises when the clues cannot be determined. Once the clues are detected it's only a matter of time before the suspects are arrested. Then comes the process of elimination, the questioning, the evaluation of the evidence, and proof, required for charging the suspected person.

After this process is completed the criminal justice system takes responsibility for the disposition of the charged individual. It is left to the courts to weigh the evidence and to acquit or convict the accused.

This investigation was still chronologically young. The motives and crimes stages had been completed and for the most part the clues had been detected but had not been correctly evaluated. Two arrests had been made and a warrant issued for Susan's arrest. Then there was the matter of Carla, she was a victim and a suspect. She would have to be arrested too, if she were still alive.

Unlike crimes, arrests are not always chronological. So far, the arrests in this case had followed a reverse chronological pattern. The last crime had been committed by Harry he had been the first to be arrested. It now appeared the second arrest, Wesley, had murdered Denny Deal.

Joe and Ray drove to 612 Magnolia, Susan's Cadillac was in the drive this time. Three times Joe rang the doorbell but got no response. He was about to open the door when Susan opened it from inside, nearly causing Joe to fall into her.

"Well, if it ain't the stranger!" She said.

"Susan I've got some bad news to lay on you."

"What is it Joe? You look so serious."

"I'm a police officer from Dallas. I am investigating the murder of Steve Stoker. Ray has something to tell you, Ray."

Ray already had his laminated Miranda warning card in his hand, along with the warrant. "Susan Jordon, I have a warrant for your arrest in connection with the murders of your husband and Steve Cranston, alias Steve Stoker. You are also wanted for questioning about the abduction of Carla Love. You have the right to remain silent..." Ray started with the constitutional rights.

For the first time since Joe had known her Joe saw fear in Susan's expression as she looked at him in disbelief. "Surely you can't believe I had anything to do with murder?"

"I'm sorry Susan it appears that you have everything to do with murder, and kidnapping," Joe said, quietly.

Susan did not cry although she appeared like she was ready to. She would not have cried even if she had understood the accusations. She had learned to control her emotions since she had been so close to all the deaths and disappointments in her life lately. She knew the only connection she had with any of this mess they were talking about was her knowledge that Steve had killed Carlton, and she could only guess about that. It was true that murder seemed to be one step behind her and everyone she had cared for had been murdered.

Back at the station Susan calmly answered Joe's questions. She had a lawyer but did not desire to have him present. "I'm sure I have nothing to hide so there's nothing to worry about. This is all a terrible mistake."

"I hope you're right Susan," said Joe.

Several hours later, after what seemed like a thousand questions, Susan had not faltered once in her answers. "I had absolutely nothing to do with Carlton's death, but I suspected Steve may have had something to do with it." Susan was very calm.

"Why didn't you go to the police?" Asked Ray.

"I've asked myself that question hundreds of times. I suppose I was so grateful to Steve for protecting me from Carlton. Then again I never had any real proof."

"What about the gun?" Joe asked.

"I swear I haven't seen Carlton's gun since I asked him to remove it from our bedroom."

"Did you give Harry Fellman instructions to kill Carla?" Asked Joe.

"Harry who?"

"Harry Fellman, the man you were talking to at your home the other night." Joe repeated the name.

Suddenly Susan recalled the incident with Harry. "I gave Harry an envelope and an attaché case for Mr. Wesley. I did not know what either contained."

"Why did you act so strange at Hogan's bar when you saw Harry that evening we went there? Joe questioned further. She seemed to be thinking then said, "Oh that, I had been in the bar several times with Bob Wesley. I knew Harry, he was a drunk. I don't like him, and I didn't want to talk to him. If we would have stayed there, he would have been at our table talking about the vacation he'd never had."

"But he had just left your house, he was there when I came by and you rushed me out of the house."

"I'm sorry about that Joe but Harry had been by the house earlier that day when I gave him the envelope. When you were there Harry had just come back to the house wanting me to give him the attaché case. I refused of course. Bob Wesley had asked me to hold it until the next day."

Joe stopped the questioning and motioned for Ray to join him outside the interview room. Once outside Joe said, "Dammit Ray, everything she says makes sense. We don't really have a damned thing on her. Either she's telling the truth or she's the best damned lying lady I've had the misfortune to meet. I'm going to let her go for now." Ray agreed and they walked back into the room.

"Susan, I'm going to let you go home now. I believe you're telling the truth, but I want you to stay around town and available until we get this mess cleared up." Joe advised her.

"Don't worry, I live and work here. Besides, I have nothing to hide," Susan assured him.

The next morning Susan called Joe's motel room before he was awake. "Hello," Joe said sleepily.

"Joe? Susan. Last night I did a lot of thinking, I couldn't sleep. Something kept bothering me then I thought of something that may help out."

"What is it?" Joe was fully awake now.

"It's just a note that showed up in the mail shortly after Carlton's death. I thought it was strange when I first saw it but never gave it much thought after that. I was going through some old cards last night and found it."

Joe dressed and got a taxi over to Susan's. What he discovered when he arrived was too good to be true. Susan handed him an envelope, addressed to Susan Jordon. There was no return address or postmark on the envelope, indicating that it had not been mailed but dropped in the mailbox by the author. Joe carefully opened the envelope and removed the single sheet of stationery;

>   *You're free now.*

>   *What are friends for.*

"Who wrote this?" Joe demanded.

"I'm not sure but I thought it may have been Steve. That was his favorite expression, 'what are friends for.' He used to say it every time he did anyone a favor." Susan became silent then she started to cry. "I suppose I always knew Steve had killed Carlton I just didn't want to admit it." Joe did not try to comfort her, she was still crying as he left, taking the note with him.

Back at the station Joe walked into the detectives' office, found Ray and threw the note onto the desk in front of him. "There's another one just like this at Carla's place. Give you any ideas?" Joe asked.

"It sure as hell does, whoever killed Carlton Jordon killed Kenny Russell too." Ray was on his feet now and ready to go. "Where to Joe?"

"Easy Ray let's get this sorted out. I'm almost positive that Steve Stoker wrote these notes. Assuming that he did would indicate that he killed or knew who killed both Jordon and Russell. If Stoker did kill both of them, then who killed Stoker?" Joe was still confused. So far it seemed he had solved every crime except the one he had come to Nashville for to begin with. This would not make Miller happy. "We have to make every effort to locate Carla Love, maybe she can explain these notes a little better."

"We've already searched the whole damned city for her Joe."

"I know Ray, but I have a feeling she's alive. We just haven't looked in the right places. We have to find her; she could very well be the last of the arrests."

Chapter Twenty
Unfinished Business

It was after midnight still Joe could not sleep. Something about the dream was not clear. He thought it odd to dream about a football jersey and the number 17 New Jersey street. He was not satisfied with finding just a handful of typewritten cards in a wastepaper basket, there had to be something more significant at that office.

Joe got out of bed and dressed. While calling for a taxi his eyes came to rest on the lonely Jack Daniel's bottles in their resting place on the table. After giving the taxi dispatcher his address, he hung up and said, "What the hell," as he picked up a bottle of the Jack Daniel's. His hands were shaking as he removed the lid and placed the bottle to his lips. After a long drink he replaced the lid and held the bottle. When the taxi arrived, Joe took the bottle with him.

Number 17 New Jersey street was dark when Joe quietly checked the entrance. It was locked, just as he expected it would be. He used his plastic driver's license to let himself into the office building and quickly ran up the stairs to the MTM records offices. Although he had subconsciously expected something, when he entered Wesley's office, he was not prepared for what he found.

The woman lying on the floor looked like Carla. She had been severely beaten, bruises all over her face and her lips were swollen. She was covered with perspiration, her clothing and the carpeted floor beneath her soaked in her sweat.

Joe shook Carla but she did not respond. He shook her harder, she opened her eyes, and jumped to her feet, screaming. "Don't kill me, please don't kill me!" When she recognized Joe, she stopped screaming, put her arms around him and would not let go. "Joe, I've been so frightened!"

"How long have you been here?" Joe asked, showing his concern.

"I don't know but it seems like forever." Carla told Joe how Wesley had brought her to the office to protect her. Joe decided that it would not be a good time to enlighten Carla to what Wesley had really planned to do to her. "Come on Carla, we're going to have you examined. I think you've been through enough for the past couple days."

Joe spent the remainder of the evening outside Carla's room at the hospital. He was not taking any chances on losing her again. Joe Ruddy would ensure that someone remained on watch outside room 308 as long as Carla was required to stay there. Too much was riding on her safety.

The next morning Carla awoke refreshed. She was still not mentally stable enough for Joe to question and he had no intentions of causing her further psychological problems. Ted Simpson had been right again, thought Joe. He had almost charged Susan with murder, now it appeared she may not be involved at all. He would be extremely careful with Carla.

Joe called Ray and asked him to arrange for two uniformed officers to guard Carla's room. When the policemen arrived, Joe returned to his motel room where, for the next twelve hours Joe Ruddy was not conscious of anything. He slept a peaceful, dreamless sleep.

That Evening Joe carefully prepared questions to ask Carla. Only a few unanswered questions remained;

1. *What did she know about Kenny Russell's death?*

2. *Did she know who had written the notes?*

3. *Did she have anything to do with the murders?*

4. *Did she know who committed the murders?*

5. *What did she know about Wesley that would make him want to kill her?*

After two days rest in the hospital Carla had almost completely recovered. Joe had decided not to arrest her unless, at some time during the questioning it became apparent she had actually committed an offense. After he explained his intentions to Carla, she agreed to answer his questions as truthfully as she could.

"I was questioned about Kenny's death because during the autopsy they found marks on his body which indicated he had been held while the drug was administered intravenously. I suppose the police thought I had something to do with it because Kenny died while he was in bed with me." Carla was silent for a few moments then Joe asked another question.

"While I was searching your house, I found a note. Do you know the one I mean?"

"You must be talking about the one about me being free, what are friends for?"

"That's the one." Joe verified.

"I suspected that Steve had written the note. That was one of his favorite expressions, he used it a lot." Carla said, as if she had been expecting the question and was relieved that it had finally been asked. "I loved Steve. He had helped me with Kenny and was so nice to me. I had never been treated the way Steve treated me." Carla told Joe the story of how she had net Steve, the lunches and everything.

"Did you know Steve killed Kenny?"

"I suspected, almost knew that he had something to do with it. He probably thought he was protecting me, that's why I had never mentioned it to anyone."

"Why were you so reluctant to talk that morning at the studio when Wesley was there?"

"Denny had called Susan, like I told you before. Well, after Susan had talked to Denny, he called again a few minutes later. He was scared and told me that Wesley had psyched him into killing Steve. He said that Wesley was constantly suggesting that he should do something about the way Steve treated him." Carla paused.

"Hold it, you're saying Denny killed Steve?" Joe asked, skeptically.

"That's what Denny said. He asked me to come to his apartment later that evening and bring Susan, he wanted to explain his situation to both of us, why he had to leave town." Carla paused again, giving Joe a chance to absorb this new insight. She had just explained the photographs taken of Susan and her together in Denny's apartment.

"So, what did Denny tell you when you got to his place?"

"He had become frightened because some man had been asking questions about Steve, that man was probably you I assumed. I was at the Western club the night you were asking the questions. Who do you think put the note on your car?" Carla asked. "That's why I was shocked when you told me you were a police officer. I still wasn't sure I could trust you until then. The reason I suspected Susan was that night at Denny's she kept saying there was no way Mr. Wesley could be involved in anything like what Denny was suggesting."

Carla got up from the sofa and offering Joe a cold drink, she went into the kitchen. A few minutes later she returned with the drinks. "I was going to tell you about all of this the night I was abducted. I was just waiting for the right time. Anyway, I left Denny's just before midnight, he'd asked me to get some groceries for him, he was afraid to go outside. When I left Denny and Susan were arguing. I couldn't have been gone more than twenty minutes. When I returned, I met Mr. Wesley in the hallway. I spoke to him and he acted very nervous. The door to Denny's apartment was open, Susan was gone and then I saw Denny. He was lying in a pool of blood on the bedroom floor. I was terrified, I had no one to go to until you got back from Richmond. I didn't know who had killed Denny, Susan or Mr. Wesley but I suspected one of them was the murderer. You know the rest of what happened." Carla was about to start crying.

Joe took her in his arms, and they sat quietly for a few minutes. His thoughts returned to a few years back to Dallas, Texas. "Okay Simpson, you've proven your point!" He said.

"What did you say?" Carla asked, puzzled.

"Oh, just talking to my advisor." Joe smiled, kissing Carla on the cheek, not wanting to hurt her injured lips. Then placing a finger to his own lips, indicating for her to remain silent, he went from room to room checking the house. He locked the doors then in an exaggerated gesture he pulled open the closet door. "Good, Harry's not here tonight," he joked.

Joe slowly walked to the sofa where Carla sat watching, on her face a confused expression. Joe smiled as he sat down beside her. Taking her in his arms once again he said, "Ms. Love, you and I have to take care of some unfinished business."

Chapter Twenty-one
You Can't Say Goodbye to A Cowboy

Carla and Joe spent the rest of the evening on the sofa and floor at 335 Washington street. The next morning Carla suggested they drive to Susan's. "I'd like to see if I still have a job," she said.

Joe said he didn't mind but first he wanted to stop by his motel room and change clothes. Before leaving Carla's, Joe called Ray at the Nashville police station. "It looks like the only ones we'll be charging are Wesley and Fellman. I'm convinced that Susan nor Carla had anything to do with the murders. I'll drop my statement off in a little while."

He quickly wrote his conclusions on an official statement form he had gotten from Ray earlier. He also wrote his Dallas phone number in case Ray needed to get in touch with him. The case would be going to court and he would have to return to Nashville to testify.

Carla and Joe left the driveway, Joe behind the wheel of Carla's Volkswagen. Their first stop was the Nashville police station where he gave Ray the statement. "I have left my address and phone number so if you ever make it to Dallas, look me up. It's been good working with you Ray, so-long." Joe shook Ray's hand firmly and left.

Their next stop was Joe's motel room where he showered then dressed in a western cut shirt, blue jeans, and a flat brimmed Stetson. Slipping his boots on he noticed Carla smiling at him. "What are you laughing at?"

"You really are a cowboy, aren't you?"

As they were leaving Joe said, "What the hell, why not?" He picked up the last two bottles of Jack Daniel's from the table, "We're all friends here, right?"

Susan was surprised to see them. She and Carla had a lot of things to talk about. It was plain to see these two girls cared for each other. Joe wandered into the kitchen and returned with three glasses. He poured Jack Daniel's and gave each of the girls a glass. "I propose a toast to the music industry!" He said.

"Joe, how about a song before we have to say goodbye?" Susan asked.

Joe picked up the Martin, checked the tune and sang a brand-new song,

> *You can't say goodbye to a cowboy*
>
> *You've just got to say so-long*
>
> *You never know when you'll see him again*
>
> *You'll never know he's leaving 'til he's gone*
>
> *You can't say goodbye to a cowboy*
>
> *Cause you just might be seeing him again*
>
> *He may not stay too long he likes to be alone*
>
> *He'll be back when you see him walk in*
>
> *You can't say goodbye to a cowboy*
>
> *And just hide him somewhere in your mind*
>
> *He may stay hid awhile but keeping with his style*
>
> *The cowboy will drift in again sometime*

After the song Joe made a quick escape. "So-long," he said, waving at Susan and Carla. He walked to Hogan's bar, ordered a double Jack Daniel's straight and thought, is this the music industry or the murder industry?

Chapter Twenty-two
Fantasy Girl

"Would you like something to drink sir?" Joe opened his eyes to see who was talking.

"Would you care for something to drink sir?" The stewardess asked again.

"Yes, Jack Daniel's and coke please," Joe said. He knew he would never stop drinking. Nashville had just made him more aware of his vices.

The Boeing 747 jet was forty minutes from the Dallas-Fort Worth airport. Captain Miller would meet him at the terminal building. I'm almost home, if I have a home, Joe thought. I suppose Dallas is as close to a home as I will ever have.

Before the stewardess had disturbed him, Joe had been dreaming. Some of his dreams lately, had been enough to confuse Freud, needless to say what affect they were having on Joe. This particular dream had not been disturbing. He considered it more along the lines of a pleasant one. He closed his eyes tightly and tried to recall the beautiful dream-girl. She had been enticing but he could not recall much about her physical appearance.

Joe removed a ballpoint from his shirt pocket and wrote:

Fantasy Girl

I've come to the conclusion that you are an illusion

You're something from some fantasy world

I can't stand the confusion when I wake up and lose you

Cause you are my fantasy girl

You're mine only when I'm dreaming

I can't have your love when I'm awake

Yes, you keep my body steaming

I don't know how much more I can take

Every time I'm ready to kiss you

That's when you tell me goodbye

Your love is always to be continued

Until I go to sleep the next time

You talk to me softly each night

But when I move to touch you, you leave

The way you treat me ain't right

I just can't wait till I go to sleep

There, he thought, that pretty much covers all that I can recall of the dream.

The 747 landed on schedule. Inside the terminal building Captain Miller was not hard to locate. Joe simply fixed his gaze above the heads of the crowd and there was Miller. The captain smiled when he saw his colleague.

"Captain, it's good to see you," said Joe.

"Same here Joe. We thought you were never going to solve that Stoker mess. Thought we had lost you to the country music industry."

"Murder industry," Joe replied.

"What's that?" Miller asked, confused.

"Oh nothing," Joe did not explain.

Most of the last month Joe had spent in Nashville on an undercover homicide investigation. It had resulted in a barrel of worms. He had uncovered and solved three other homicides, all the victims and suspects had been involved in the music industry. Joe had sarcastically termed it the murder industry since he had left Nashville.

Joe followed the big captain outside the terminal building to the waiting, unmarked police vehicle. They got into the car and Joe brought Miller up to date on the conclusions he had reached in Nashville. The Stoker/Cranston homicide had been solved. When he had completed his oral report Miller said, "It sounds like you've been busy. But I knew we were sending the right man for the job."

"Thanks for the praise Captain, but it's sure good to be home."

Miller opened the glove compartment and removed Joe's shield and .9 mm Smith & Wesson, automatic. "I suppose that you'll be needing these now that your home."

"Possibly," Joe said, accepting the gun and badge. "Does this mean that I go right back to the old grind?"

"I'm afraid so. We're shorthanded at the detective division right now," said Miller apologetically.

Interstate 35 was crowded; it was a hot day and Joe was tired. Just before they turned off the interstate Joe noticed a lady in the back seat of a late model Chevrolet. As the police car, in which Joe was riding, passed the Chevy, Joe glanced inside the other car. The lady was sitting alone in the rear seat while two rough looking men were in the front seat.

She looks familiar but where have I seen her before? Joe thought. Out of habit he jotted the license plate number in his notebook.

"What are you doing Joe?"

"I'm going to check something out. The occupants of that Chevy look suspicious."

"It looks perfectly normal to me," said Miller.

"Yea, but I've got a feeling about it Captain. Something ain't quite right." Captain Miller shook his head and giggled as he turned the sedan off the interstate.

Joe had a strange feeling as he looked at the familiar police station. He had experienced unforgettably wild evenings in this old building. Memories that he cherished were revived momentarily. Miller parked in the police parking lot. Both men got out of the car and walked inside.

"You'll be glad to know that I haven't assigned you any new cases since you've been gone this month Joe."

"Good Captain, I have that back log that I need to start working on anyway," Joe said, thankfully.

Joe was conversing with his captain, but he was concentrating on the Chevrolet. He barely knew what he was saying to Miller. He told Captain Miller that he would meet him upstairs in a few minutes. Then removing his notebook, he walked to the traffic division. "Hey Mike, could you run a make on this license plate for me?" Joe asked, handing Mike his notebook.

"Sure, Joe be glad to," Mike answered, accepting the battered notebook. He jotted the plate number down and returned the book to Joe. "Give me about thirty minutes. I'll call you when I get an answer. You're gonna be topside, right?"

"Yea, I have a feeling that I'm going to be topside for a long time." Joe was pleased to be back in Dallas.

Joe was not a full-time homicide detective like Captain Miller. He was a general detective therefore he was likely to be assigned to any number of varied cases, at any time. There was one consolation-it was not as bad as being stuck in a rut, doing the same type of investigations day in and day out.

Since joining the Dallas police department three years ago Joe had been assigned as a traffic policeman, the vice squad, robbery division, narcotics, homicide and had dabbled in burglary and larceny. So far, he had not been assigned the riot and crowd control detail.

Joe slowly climbed the stairs to the detective bureau. He knew that a pile of paperwork awaited him at his desk. Maybe one day he would learn to not detest the paperwork that was inevitable at the conclusion of any investigation. But today he could not get motivated.

At noon he was still shuffling paper and had not decided which case to start on. All of the investigations were old and had no leads. Typical of the cases he had been assigned since he had joined the detectives. That was only one of the disadvantages of being the newest detective on the force. He caught all the cases the veterans didn't want. For Joe to come up with the slightest lead he had to spend hours of leg work and sit through countless interviews. Joe's patience had paid off over the years though. He had solved over one hundred cases as a military police investigator.

He finally decided on his next investigation. He opened the folder. Dammit this frigging thing is five years old, he thought. Why had no one bothered to ask questions on this case? He thumbed through the complaint, reading the synopsis;

Alleged Extortion (attempted)

Victim-Andrea Peters

Peters reported that an unknown male had called her home and   demanded she pay him $20,000.00. If she refused to pay him, he threatened to make public some information that could harm her financially. She could not or would not disclose any further information. No action can be taken on this investigation until Peters provides further information…

It was Joe's duty to make a determination on these old cases. If he could not develop leads, then he was to close the less serious ones. He laid the Peters' case aside.

Mike, from the traffic division called a few minutes later. "Joe I've got the make on the Chevy. Plate number HZ-4095. You can pick the sheet up anytime."

"Thanks Mike," said Joe.

Joe mechanically walked downstairs, picked up the BMV sheet and returned to his desk. Sitting down, he scanned it.

1983 Chevrolet, License plate #HZ-4095

Registered to-CAREY, William

Address—315 Montgomery Ave., Dallas, Texas

At 3:00 P.M. Joe said goodbye to Miller, placed the Peters' folder under his arm and walked outside to his Charger. He was going to drive over to Montgomery. He would stop off there on his way home.

Checking the numbers as he slowly cruised Montgomery avenue, Joe stopped in front of number 315. It was a rental unit, managed by Slater realty, according to the sign posted in the front lawn. The house was not occupied presently. He parked the Charger in the driveway, got out and walked to the front of the house. Joe checked the front door it was secured with a dead bolt lock. He tried the side entrance, but it too was locked. He was able to insert his plastic credit card into the jamb enough to release the cheap locking mechanism. The door opened easily as he pushed against it.

Joe nearly fell over a trash can filled with empty beer cans as he tried to maintain his balance stumbling through the door. He made a quick walk through inspection. The house was void of furniture. The trash can was the only thing left by the former tenants. Then as he opened the door to a bedroom at the rear of the house, he saw something.

Panty hose? Lying in the closet was a pair of ladies' panty hose. Panty hose was not what Joe had hoped to discover. His curiosity would not have been aroused except for the knots that had been tied in both the silk legs. He picked the garment up from the floor and scrutinized it for some time. The hose had been cut. This was all Joe needed to activate his wild imagination. There had been a crime committed in this house recently. Joe didn't know the nature of the crime, but he could sense that some unlawful act had occurred here.

He stuffed the panty hose into his jacket pocket and returned to the kitchen. His hand was on the doorknob then he stopped, walked over to the trash can and kicked the container. It fell over, banging against the floor with a loud crash. Empty beer cans rolled across the tiled floor. Just beer cans, he thought. Then Joe saw an old newspaper.

He rescued the newspaper from the aluminum mess, it was soaked with beer. He observed that some of the beer cans still had a small amount of beer remaining in them. The occupants have not been gone too long, he thought.

The date on the newspaper was only a week old. Joe could not help noticing that someone had outlined an article in red ink. He read the article.

Andrea Peters, heiress to the James Peters' estate had proven her claim to the inheritance valid. After five years of costly court room battles, it appears that Miss Peters has convinced the courts that she is entitled to the multi-million-dollar estate. Miss Peters' was not available for comment but has agreed to make a public statement concerning her rags to riches story in the Sunday edition of this newspaper.

Joe hastily searched the front page hoping to find more on the story. Nothing there. He rolled the newspaper and tucking it securely under his arm, left the house.

Next door to 315 Montgomery, he rang the doorbell and waited impatiently. A few minutes later an elderly lady opened the door.

"Good afternoon ma'am," said Joe, showing her his shield. "I'm with the Dallas police department. Could you tell me when the people moved from the house next door?"

"You mean Mister Carey?"

"Yes ma'am, 315," Joe pointed to the house in question.

"They moved out of there a couple of days ago, but I saw him right back over there early this morning." The old lady paused briefly. "He and some other young feller were in the car. I thought it was peculiar though, because when I saw them leave there was a girl with them."

"A girl?" Joe asked.

"Yes, and she appeared to be injured or something. The gentleman that was with Mr. Carey was helping her into the back seat of the car."

"Was Carey a good neighbor?" Joe inquired.

"He was until a few weeks ago. He was a bachelor and didn't spend much time at home you know. Then he started having these loud, wild parties. Last week was the worst one though."

"What do you mean?" Joe asked.

"About two o'clock in the morning a noise woke me. It was screams. I walked outside and sure enough I heard the screams again. They were coming from Mr. Carey's house. I called the police, but they never did come out. About three o'clock I went back to bed. The screams had stopped."

Joe thanked the lady and left. Back in the car he thought, thank goodness for nosy little old ladies. Joe backed the car out of the driveway and headed towards the 3rd street library. He wanted to check last Sunday's newspaper.

The librarian was a young, cheerful lady in her early twenties. She looked nothing like the typical librarian was supposed to look-eyeglasses, hair pulled into a bun. She was almost attractive, Joe thought.

"May I help you sir?" The voice was a sexy, low Texas drawl.

"Yes, I would like to see a back issue of the Dallas Ledger."

"Any particular date you wish to see?"

"Last Sunday please," Joe said. The librarian removed last Sunday's paper from the rack and handed it to Joe. "Here you are sir."

"Thanks," Joe took the paper.

It didn't take him long to locate the article. When he turned to the third page the picture of Miss Peters nearly jumped from the page. He had been so concerned with finding some answers to why the Chevrolet had seemed so suspicious, then it suddenly snapped. Andrea Peters was the victim of the old case he had chosen to investigate.

When he saw the picture in the newspaper Joe could not contain himself. "That's her! That's her!" He shouted. Then he suddenly remembered where he was and stopped shouting. The girl whose picture he was staring at this very moment and the girl in the Chevrolet were one in the same. But that was not what had caused his excitement. He had suspected that since finding the newspaper at 315 Montgomery. What Joe was so excited about was the girl in the newspaper, the girl in the Chevy, and the victim in the five-year-old extortion case were all Andrea Peters, his fantasy girl.

Chapter Twenty-Three
Reasons to Stay

She had spent her life, all nineteen years of it, in virtual poverty. Her mother had told her several times that Andrea's father, James Peters, was a wealthy man. She had hated her father for leaving when she had been nine weeks old, she nor her mother had heard from him since.

Andrea's mother had died two weeks ago, leaving her alone in Toledo to deal with a cruel world. Andrea, not knowing where to turn, had saved her money and come to Dallas. She had heard that her father was in the oil business here.

The two-day ride on the Greyhound bus had exhausted her, she had been sleeping when she faintly heard the driver's voice, "Dallas, Texas. The bus will be reloading in thirty minutes."

Andrea got off the bus and went inside where she claimed her luggage, two battered, unmatched suitcases. She had no idea where to start looking for her father, but what was worse, she didn't know if he would accept her if she was lucky enough to find him. Presenting the baggage clerk her claim, she picked up her suitcases and drudged off to the snack counter.

Andrea sat down at a table and counted her money, $46.00, that's all she had to survive on in this city of strangers. She ordered a coke from the impatient waitress who scampered off to get the drink. Andrea couldn't spend too much she would have to have a place to sleep tonight.

Andrea did not know that she was three weeks late in her attempt to locate her father. A cardiac arrest had suddenly ended his life. She would soon discover that her father had not forgotten her, deserted her maybe, but he had not forgotten his daughter. Andrea was a stranger in Dallas today but soon she would become the object of anger, resentment, and hate, for at this very moment in a classier section of Dallas some of

James Peters' loving relatives were plotting to own the Peters' estate.

Andrea rented a cheap motel room and slept for ten hours. When she awoke, she found the telephone book and searched for James Peters' phone number. Her father was not listed in the directory but while she had thumbed absently through the yellow pages, she glanced at an ad for Peters' Petroleum Research. Why not? Her father was supposed to be in the oil business.

She dialed the number anxiously, "Peters' Petroleum Research, may I help you?" was the pleasant greeting.

Not knowing what to say she stuttered, "Aha...aha...this is Andrea Peters. I'm from out of town and I'm here in Dallas trying to locate my father. Could you tell me if James Peters is the owner of your company?"

"He was the owner. I'm afraid Mr. Peters passed away three weeks ago." The gloomy reply frightened Andrea. "Are you still there miss?"

"What? Yes, I'm here, go on," Andrea whispered.

"I'm Laura, formerly Mr. Peters' private secretary. Your father's death has created quite a problem here at the Research center. In his will he has bequeathed his entire estate to his daughter Andrea, the problem is no one knew of her existence."

"What did you say?" Andrea could not believe what she was hearing.

"What I'm saying is, if you are the Andrea Peters then you are a very wealthy young lady. Your father's estate was estimated at more than 10 million dollars," Laura finished.

It had been five years now since Andrea had arrived in Dallas and learned of her wealth. She had not seen one penny of the money until ten days ago. She'd had to prove to the courts that she was James Peters' daughter and not a fraud. Now that she did have the estate, which had ultimately totaled

12 million dollars, she could not enjoy it. She had stayed at the Peters' mansion for only six nights. Now here she was, drugged and tied, being hauled across Texas by two thugs she did not know.

It was almost hopeless to investigate a crime this old, but Joe was an optimist. If Andrea had received no other threatening calls over the past five years, chances were the extortionist would never call again. It was nearing sunset when he stopped his Charger in front of the Peters' mansion in Arlington park.

Walking up to the plantation style mansion Joe admired the tall columns and the landscape around the humble abode. As he stepped onto the marble decking of the porch he nearly slipped on the slick surface. Joe pushed the button by the door and was charmed by a pleasant chime sounding from somewhere inside the house. A few seconds later a neatly dressed black woman answered the door.

"May I help you sir?" She inquired.

"I'm here to see Andrea Peters please," Joe said, showing the maid his shield.

"I'm sorry but Ms. Peters has not been here in four days."

"When is she expected to return?" Joe asked.

"She didn't tell us anything, we don't even know where she is. I noticed that her car is in the garage though."

"Has she left like this before?"

"I couldn't say sir, Ms. Andrea, she only stayed here a week. It looks to me like she would have left some kind of message." The maid's face was starting to show a worried expression.

Joe thanked the housekeeper and returned to his car. He didn't know much about Andrea Peters, just what he'd read in the papers actually, but he couldn't imagine her disappearing like this. It appears to me, Joe thought, that Andrea had 12 million reasons to stay. Joe's Charger was parked in the circular drive for another fifteen minutes while he wrote;

Reasons to Stay

I read it in a magazine

Heard it on the radio

The papers said the same thing

But how could they know

Cause you didn't tell anyone you were going

I don't think you knew till you were on your way

And maybe that wasn't your face they were showing

Or it could be you ran out of reasons to stay

Did I really find a note

Saying what you had to say

A list of things you wrote

Were they all reasons to stay

I'm sorry you had to go

Could have been till we were gray

But I guess we didn't know

You'd run out of reasons to stay

Chapter Twenty-Four
Officer Down

At 7:30 P.M. Don Vander, the one and only policeman in the small town of Savoy, Texas, stopped by his house to have a cold drink. "It's a scorcher out there tonight mama," Don said to his wife Lucille.

"Why don't you call it a night? It's been quiet all night anyway," she coaxed.

"Honey, I'd like to, but I better run the radar a few more hours. The wild drivers will be coming through here about nine. I've got to try to keep this town safe for our children." Don took a large swallow of the iced tea Lucille had just sat on the table.

He had been a dedicated policeman for twenty-five years. The last five years he had spent here in Savoy. After he had retired from the Dallas police force, he had wanted to settle down in a quiet place and raise his family. Don kissed his wife and told her that he'd be home soon.

Don got into the police cruiser and drove to the center of Savoy. He backed the car into the parking lot by the Shell gas station and turned off the engine and headlights. Turning on the doppler radar system, Don adjusted the antennae and set the audible alarm. He leaned back in the seat and closed his tired eyes.

He was proud of the new radar equipment he had persuaded the city council to buy only three months before. Don had already written enough legitimate traffic citations to pay for the radar installation.

At about 9:15 P.M. he was ready to call it a night then the radar alarm sounded. A late model Chevrolet headed east on highway 78 was breaking the posted speed limit. Eighty in a fifty zone, that'll cost him about a hundred dollars, thought Don.

The car did not slow down as it entered the small town. Don leaned forward and started the engine. As the speeding car passed the cruiser Don flipped the switch to activate the overhead lights and pursued the Chevy. After about a quarter mile chase the Chevy stopped. Don quickly recorded the license plate number as he eased the cruiser in behind the Chevy and parked.

Cautiously Don walked to the driver's side of the car, looking into the back seat. There he saw a young lady lying on the seat, apparently sleeping. The two men in the front seat were obviously nervous but so was Don. At times like these a cop needed a patrol partner.

"Sir, I stopped you for a speeding violation. You were clocked by radar at eighty in a fifty zone. I'll need your driver's license and registration please." Don was polite.

The driver said, "Yes officer, I realize that I was speeding." Then he made a movement as if reaching for his wallet. Don, keeping his eyes on the driver, did not notice as the other male occupant in the front seat raised the sawed-off double-barreled Savage and fired.

As he fell to the pavement Don could see the Chevy speed away. He wanted to crawl to the cruiser and call Lucille on the citizen's band-she always monitored the CB until he came home-but he did not have the strength.

Lucille had heard the blast and reacted quickly. She tried to contact Don on the CB. When she got no response, she ran to the neighbor's house. "Could you ride over to the gas station and check on Don? He won't answer the CB and I heard what sounded like gunfire from that direction. I think something may be wrong with him." She tried to act calm, but Lucille was visibly shaken.

The neighbor, Mr. Wilson, asked no questions as he pulled on his boots, ran to his pickup and drove to where Don usually parked. The police cruiser was not there. Wilson looked to the east and could barely see the flashing blue lights. He drove toward the lights.

As he neared the police cruiser Wilson slowed his pickup. He thought it odd that only the police car would be sitting by the road-he expected to see a car that Don had pulled over. At first Don was nowhere to be seen then Wilson caught a glimpse of his nearly lifeless body, lying on the paved portion of the road. He slammed the brake pedal hard, jumped from the truck and ran to Don's side. Wilson grabbed the injured policeman's wrist and checked for a pulse, any sign of life. There was a faint pulse, but time was running out for Don Vander.

There was no time to waste, Wilson lifted Don's limp body and half carried, half drug him to the police cruiser. Frantically Wilson settled himself behind the wheel and drove to Bonham, the nearest hospital, twelve miles to the east.

Ten minutes later he parked the cruiser at the emergency room entrance, he had never driven that fast in his entire life. Wilson excitedly ran inside and told the duty nurse what had happened as the attendants brought Don inside. He was still alive, but his condition was critical.

When Wilson had settled down some, he called his home. Mrs. Wilson answered the phone. "Jay, where are you? You've had us scared to death!" She exclaimed.

"I had to rush Don to the hospital in Bonham, he's hurt bad. It appears that he has been shot with a shotgun. He's still alive though so don't get Lucille excited. Tell her that I'll come by and pick her up. You go ahead and get their young'uns brought over to the house."

Jay Wilson drove the police cruiser back to Savoy, resisting the urge to break the speed limit on the way. When he got to the house to get Lucille Vander she was crying. He tried to comfort her but was not experienced in these matters and could not find the right things to say. Finally, he decided on his best line, "Don's going to be alright Lucille.

Chapter Twenty-Five
Honkytonk Star

Joe had not called Julie since he had returned from Nashville, where the Stoker homicide case had kept him for the past month. He wanted to surprise her so at 9:00 P.M. he parked his Charger in the Torn Dollar parking lot. Reaching into the back seat he removed a bottle of Jack Daniel's he had bought earlier that day. Joe sat quietly for a few minutes sipping from the bottle. He had not planned on getting attached to Julie, or anyone for that matter, but that night they'd spent in the motel room over a month ago had aroused Joe's masculinity.

He entered the Torn Dollar a few minutes later and took a seat near the end of the bar. Julie was busy waiting on customers when she noticed Joe, smiling she came to him. "Joe, it's good to see you!" She made no attempt to conceal her excitement.

"It's good to be back Julie," Joe said. "Where's the band?"

"We don't have a band on Thursdays anymore." She placed the Jack Daniel's on the bar in front of Joe then resting her chin in the palm of her hand, elbow on the bar, she stared affectionately at him.

"What time do you close?"

"Two."

Joe checked his Timex, "I'd like to take you home tonight, but I have some things to do. I'll stop in again before closing time." He knew if he stayed at the bar for five hours, he would not be able to take Julie anywhere. He would be lucky to be able to walk after slugging down Jack Daniel's for five hours.

Julie consented with a smile. She was lovely, her pale complexion, red hair and green eyes, what had attracted Joe to her in the first place, was shadowed in the dim light of the nightclub. She placed her hand over his and their eyes met. Without words they communicated.

Joe reluctantly raised his glass and finished the drink in one gulp. As he stood, he said apologetically. "I really do have some things that have to be done tonight."

"I believe you. I'll see you at about one." Julie laughed.

It was 10:00 P.M. when Joe entered the Dallas PD parking lot. Thursday nights were normally slow for crime, with the weekend near, criminals were resting. He thought it unusual to see Miller's old Ford still parked in the lot at this time of night.

Joe ran up the flight of stairs to the detective bureau, Captain Miller was in his office. As Joe entered Miller raised his head but did not speak.

"What's keeping you at the office this late Captain?"

"Don Vander has been shot Joe. I just got the word about fifteen minutes ago."

"Who got shot?" Joe had not heard the name.

"Don Vander, he was a policeman here for about twenty years and a damned good one too. He retired about five years ago and has been a policeman in Savoy, Texas since then. That's a little town about a hundred miles northeast of here." Miller explained softly.

"How did it happen?"

"The state boys are investigating that right now. So far the only thing they have to go on is a license plate number that was found in Don's notebook."

"Have they run a make on it yet?"

"They're doing that now, the shooting just happened thirty-five minutes ago." Miller snapped.

"How did you find out so fast?"

"Lucille Vander called, we were all good friends, she and my wife and Don and I, she notified me because she didn't know who to turn to." Miller explained then became silent again.

"Do you have the plate number?"

Miller nodded and pushed a note pad across his desk so Joe could read it. As soon as he saw the numbers he knew, "Oh shit, Captain! This is the same damned vehicle I saw on I-35 today." Joe briefed Miller on the details of the investigation he had just started hours ago.

"Get with the state boys and let them know what you've already got on Carey. If they request your assistance, we'll assign you to them." Miller instructed.

Andrea Peters had created another mystery for Joe to become involved in. He could only hope that it would not become as bloody as the one in Nashville had been. He was not anticipating another long, drawn-out investigation this soon after his Music City experience.

Joe remained at the station talking with Miller until after midnight. They swapped at least a dozen war stories reminiscing about their old days in Germany. But Joe had a more enjoyable evening planned with Julie. He said goodnight to Miller and left the captain to his thoughts of his old friend Don Vander.

There were very few customers remaining at the Torn Dollar. With all the new nightclubs springing up all over Dallas it was not lucrative for an old honkytonk to stay in business. Years before Joe had moved to Dallas the Torn Dollar had probably been one of the most popular night spots along this strip. It was one of thirty or so clubs constructed in the early '50's along Houston Boulevard. Most of the other clubs had long since been razed but somehow the Torn Dollar had survived the reconstruction.

In the '70's the disco scene urbanized the night crowds, moving them back into city clubs like the club 51, to mention only one.

Faithful Julie was on her way towards him with a Jack Daniel's in hand. As she set his drink on the bar she said, "I've been expecting you to call and tell me you couldn't make it, or that something had come up. All those standard lines."

"Well, something did come up but that's all the more reason for me to make it back tonight." Joe winked, then impatiently asked, "Are we going to your place or mine?"

Julie playfully slapped his arm then said, "It will be your place, I live with my mother and I don't think she would appreciate me bringing someone home at this hour."

"That's fine by me but I must warn you my place is probably a mess." Joe admitted.

They arrived at Joe's apartment about 3:00 A.M. and the place was a mess. He had not remembered leaving the kitchen in such disarray. When he found the coffee grounds Julie started the automatic coffee maker. Joe went into the other room and returned a few minutes later with his guitar. As he began to strum the instrument, he told Julie about his trip to Nashville. He became serious as his fingers fondled the strings of the Ovation. "You know, I guess I'll never be anything but a cop and occasionally a honkytonk star." He began to sing, making the lyrics up as he went;

>*Honkytonk Star*
>
>*I never gave it any thought it never crossed my mind*
>
>*It was not important if you drink you've seen the kind*
>
>*Jukebox in the corner some tables, stools and bar*
>
>*If there were no honkytonks, I wouldn't be a star*
>
>*I'm a honkytonk star I sound better when I've had a few*
>
>*I'm a honkytonk star it helps if you've had some too*
>
>*If I forget the songs, it's a short trip to the bar*
>
>*Then it jogs my memory I'm a honkytonk star*

*I don't sign no autographs I know most of you by
name*

If I see you tomorrow, you know I'll be the same

I don't want the big time I like this atmosphere

I'm a honkytonk star that started out right here

"That's real good Joe," Julie said when he had finished the song. "Why don't you come over to the club some night and do a show?"

Joe smiled, "I don't have that much time off."

"I could talk to the owner maybe we could get you in next Thursday. Would you do it?"

"Sure, I'd love to."

As they drank coffee and quietly talked Joe felt cozy and wanted this time with Julie to last forever but he would have to get some sleep soon. They both knew why Julie had come to Joe's apartment. Without a word Joe stood and removed his shirt. Taking the cue Julie also stood and said, "Unzip me please."

As he unzipped the back of her short black dress, he saw that she was not wearing a bra, but she didn't need one, her breasts were large but firm. Joe could not resist the urge as his hands slipped inside the garment to fondle Julie's breasts. He felt the hardened nipples burning his hands. Julie was ready when Joe removed his hands and let the dress fall to the floor. She was facing him as he took her in his arms and kissed her roughly on the lips. They were silent as he lifted her in his arms and carried her to the bed where they made love until they both fell asleep.

Joe did not need an alarm clock, Miller usually made sure that he never overslept. He didn't know how many times the phone had rung before he answered it.

"Joe meet me at the station in half an hour. The state boys say they want you and me both on this cop shooting!" Miller was excited.

"Okay Captain, I'm on my way." Joe had not opened his eyes yet. He shook Julie, who was lying with her arms tightly hugging a pillow. "Julie, I'm leaving, do you want me to set the alarm?"

"No, I just want to sleep and think about last night."

As Joe dressed, he looked at his Timex, it was only 7:30 A.M., why had Miller called so early? Before leaving the apartment, Joe checked Julie once more. She was sleeping soundly and did not stir as he kissed her lightly on the lips.

He arrived at the station ten minutes before Captain Miller. It had been awhile since Miller had worked the streets he had been confined to the office as an administrator. He was excited about going out with Joe on this investigation. When he walked into the office Miller removed his jacket and hung it on the coat hook. Joe looked up from the morning newspaper to see Miller, wearing a shoulder holster that cradled a shiny new .44 magnum. He also wore a snub nosed .38 in a butterfly holster, tucked inside the rear waistband of his trousers.

Joe said, "Going hunting Captain?"

"Goddamned right I'm going hunting, cop killers. Don was a friend of mine I'm going to find the scum that gunned him down." Miller paced around the office nervously. Finally, the big captain sat down at his desk, propped both feet up on the edge of it and asked, "Okay Joe, what have you got on these assholes?"

"The car is a 1983 Chevrolet registered to William Carey. He did reside at 315 Montgomery. I checked the place out, it's a rental. According to one of the neighbors Carey is a bachelor and he moved out of the house earlier this week, probably Monday."

"Is that all you have?"

"It's only a hunch but I would say that Carey and another unknown male are holding Andrea Peters for ransom. I believe there were three people in the car that Vander stopped last night. We need to do some digging here in Dallas and find out who Carey's cohort is."

"Who is this Andrea Peters?" Miller wanted to know.

"She just inherited 12 million dollars," Joe explained.

"Let's get an NCIC Check on Carey. Check our files too. Find out where he works, who his friends are… When we go up against this pair, I want to know what I'm facing." Miller was like a child with a new toy he had not been this actively involved in an investigation in more than two years.

By noon the day after Don Vander had been blasted with the shotgun Joe knew the identity of the second passenger in Carey's Chevy. It was quite by accident that he had stumbled onto this bit of information. After several phone calls Joe learned that Carey had been employed by Peters' Petroleum Products. They drove out to the place.

Joe and Miller arrived at the Peters' offices just before noon. At the reception area just inside the modern building they were directed to the personnel office on the second floor.

"Yes, Mister Carey worked for the company for about six years. We had to let him go about four years ago," explained the friendly blonde lady behind the desk.

"What was the reason for his termination?" Joe asked.

"Just a moment, I'll pull his file."

The lady got up from the desk and walked to the back of the long office. She said something to another, younger woman who was seated at a large desk. In front of her was a complex computer system with thousands of buttons and knobs. She pushed several of those buttons and a printer hummed for a few seconds.

The blonde lady returned to the front of the office and handed Joe a printed sheet of paper. "I thought I remembered

Carey. He was an economic geologist who did a lot of soil research for us during the late '70's. We slowed down our research projects after Mr. Peters' death and terminated several of our professional employees."

The blonde was very helpful, Joe told her so and thanked her as he and Miller started to leave.

"Carey's friend was terminated at the same time if that's any help."

Joe and Miller both stopped and smiled at each other. "What did you say?" Joe asked.

"Carey's friend, Mr. Lansky, he was released from the company at the same time."

"Is it possible to get a computer readout on him also?"

"Sure," she said and walked to the monstrous computer once more.

When she returned to the front Joe asked, "Do you by chance have a description of Carey and Lansky?"

"I can do better than that, excuse me again please." She was very polite. This time she left the office and was gone for several minutes. When she returned, she handed Joe a paper folder. He looked inside the dossier and smiled at her.

"We require photographs of all our employees for security reasons. They are a bit old but should give you some Idea of what they look like."

"These will do fine," Joe said, "Thanks."

They were the same two men Joe had seen in the Chevy yesterday. He and Miller had done about all they could do in Dallas. For now, it was just hang around and wait for the Chevy to be located. Half the law enforcement officers in east Texas were searching for Carey and Lansky now, they would turn up before long.

"Let's get these photographs aired on the news, the sooner we find them the better," Miller said.

On his way to his apartment Joe thought about Julie. He could feel the attachment becoming stronger, but he was not ready for total commitment yet. He was sure Julie felt the same was about him so for now they would just remain friends and try to not become too serious.

Joe hardly recognized his apartment when he opened the door and stepped inside. Julie had cleaned the kitchen, made the bed and arranged everything neatly. When he saw the note lying on the bed, he picked it up and read it;

> *Dear Joe,*
>
> *I had a wonderful time just wish you didn't have*
>
> *To work all the time. See you at the Torn Dollar,*
>
> *Cause you are my Honkytonk star.*
>
> *Love, Julie*

Chapter Twenty-Six
Rich Man, Poor Man, Digger Man, Thief

A lot of things can transform a law-abiding man into a criminal-the desire for wealth; will to survive; and revenge- to name just three. Some criminals will admit they became involved with crime quite accidentally. Most criminals fall into two categories- professional and impulsive criminals. A professional criminal may take pride in his modus operandi and usually carefully plans his crime. On the other hand, an impulsive criminal does not have a plan of action. This category of criminal usually commits a crime on the spur of the moment.

William Carey and Thomas Lansky were impulsive criminals. They had been friends for ten years after meeting one hot afternoon in Austin, Texas. Carey had been looking for a prospective section of earth in which to do his digging when he chose a spot next to another young Geology student- Thomas Lansky. Both men were in their early twenties and were doing their thesis for their master's degree.

Carey said, "What have you found this morning, dinosaurs, fossils or what?"

"Nothing significant," replied Lansky, "just an ancient Neanderthal tomahawk." Both men laughed.

"Mind if I join you?"

"Be my guest," Lansky invited.

Carey and Lansky spent the rest of that summer together, becoming inseparable friends. They worked, studied and partied together. When summer ended, they agreed to keep in touch. Carey returned to Dallas where he joined the research team at Peters' Petroleum Products. Early in 1974 he persuaded the staff at the research center to hire his good friend Thomas Lansky.

For six years they were employed at the research center. Never once thinking about the security of their positions, they squandered their lucrative salaries lavishly, their savings amounting to very little. Late in 1979, they were totally unprepared for the letters they received from the research center discharging their services. Since then they had been getting by, working odd jobs. There was no great demand in the job market for geologists who would rather be playboys.

In '81 Carey and Lansky were digging again. It was an expedition to Antarctica at the expense of the U.S. Government. They had been selected as part of the research team to make a study of the oil possibilities in that region. They managed to last two years in the cold weather but both men longed for the sunshine and nightlife which were nonexistent in the Antarctic.

Shortly after their return to Dallas Lansky had a brilliant idea which he discussed with Carey. They met at the golf course for their usual Saturday morning of 18 holes.

"You know," said Lansky, "I don't see why we should do without the finer things of life. We're not stupid, we're both college graduates. I think we should direct our knowledge towards a career in crime."

Carey laughed. Then Lansky, very seriously, removed a small leather pouch from his pocket. "Take a look at these babies," he said, opening the pouch and pouring out a handful of brilliantly colored gems.

"Where did you get those?" Bill asked, on his face an expression of surprise.

"At the home of some filthy rich bastard who probably will not discover them missing for days. I just walked into the house last night and walked out with a pouch full of gems. I can get rid of them before they are reported stolen." Lansky smiled.

"They must be worth at least a hundred grand!" Carey estimated. The golf game forgotten they left the golf course to have a drink and discuss Lansky's proposition further.

They dabbled in burglary for the next year not doing more than three jobs, just enough to finance their lavish lifestyles.

Both men agreed that stealing rocks was much easier than digging them.

On a summer morning in '84 Bill Carey was seated at the kitchen table at his rented home on Montgomery. It was early, the coffee had just finished brewing. Bill poured himself a cup of the strong mud and returned to the table to read the Dallas Ledger. One particular article caught his interest. So, they finally settled that inheritance claim. Twelve million dollars was too much money for a snot-nosed brat to be in control of. Maybe he and Lansky should relieve her of some of that cash.

He laughed as he dialed Lansky's phone number. What had amused Carey was an old saying he'd heard as a child- "Rich man, poor man, beggar man, thief..."- he and Lansky met that description with the exception of the "beggar man", they would never do that.

He changed the quote in his mind, "Richman, poor man, digger man, thief...", totally appropriate for two Geologists who had been up and down the ladder of success.

Chapter Twenty-Seven
Civic Duty

Don Vander was conscious but remained in critical condition though lucky to be alive. Not many people survived a shotgun blast at close range. He did not recognize Captain John Miller. Miller's eyes began to fill with tears as he reflected on the old days, he and Don had spent together on the Dallas PD. They had been patrol partners for five years. Miller rubbed his eyes and said, "Let's go Joe. I can't stand to see him like this. We've got to get out there and find those assholes before someone else gets hurt."

"I'm all for that Captain," Joe agreed.

The detectives left the hospital room, Miller glanced at Don and shook his head. He thought, a good man nearly shot to death in the line of duty. Nobody cares anymore.

The Bonham police department was located on a hill on the east side of the city. The department was efficient and capable of investigating any crime. Bonham's chief of police liked to boast that despite not having all the latest technological police equipment his department still had sufficient equipment and expertise to complete any task the larger departments were capable of. Texas Public Safety officer, Frank Lewis was waiting for Miller at the Bonham PD.

"Captain Miller, I'm Frank Lewis, DPS, I thought you'd like to know we have located the vehicle in Sherman. We have it under surveillance at this time."

"How far is Sherman?" Asked Miller.

"Thirty-five miles northwest of here," answered Lewis.

"Let's go Joe-Frank call your unit in Sherman and tell them we're on the way. If the suspects are arrested hold them at the Sherman PD." Miller was barking instructions he had taken complete control of the investigation.

Joe knew John Miller very well; the captain had not been this enthusiastic about police work for a long time. Joe suspected that Miller wanted revenge for Don Vander. He would not allow Miller to lose control, Joe must keep a vigilant eye on his captain.

In Joe's Charger, headed west on a country highway Miller was the first to speak. "Step on it, Joe. I wanna be there when the sons-a-bitches walk back to that car. I wanna see it when they try to resist arrest so I can test fire this new .44 magnum." Miller patted the bulge under his left arm.

The '83 Chevrolet was parked at a pay lot on the north side of Sherman the DPS unit patiently waited across the street. There had only been one customer enter the parking lot in the last two hours, an old lady returning for her car.

Miller was the first to recognize the unmarked DPS vehicle as he directed, "Pull in behind them." Joe parked behind the state car without comment. Miller exited the Charger and approached the street side of the surveillance car, showing the officer his shield, he asked, "Any sign of them yet?"

"No, we've been here since two this afternoon and no one has touched the vehicle."

"Did anyone check the bus stations, car lots or car rentals? Maybe they ditched the Chevy," Miller offered.

The two officers looked at each other, then the driver said, "It never occurred to us that they may not return for the vehicle."

Miller and Joe had not worked the streets as a team for a long time. As they started the tedious task of locating Carey and Lansky they would soon know if they could still function effectively together. Within an hour they had checked every place in the small town that offered a means of transportation for the criminals. No one remembered seeing anyone matching the descriptions of the two men. Someone in Sherman had the answer, Carey and Lansky had not evaporated, someone had seen them and had provided them with a means of escape, but who?

Sparky Stillman had lived in Sherman, Texas since his discharge from the army after WWII. He was well liked by his neighbors and well noted for his civic contributions. He was the little league coach and a voluntary policeman and fireman.

Sparky had not seen his sister, Flo's boy in over ten years so naturally he had been surprised when Bill Carey had stopped by the house this morning. Bill had always been a good boy, went to college and had never been in any kind of trouble that Sparky knew of so understandably, Sparky had not hesitated to loan his nephew the old Volkswagen. Now, as he was about to eat his supper, he sat at the table and said, "Carolyn turn the tube on."

Carolyn, Sparky's wife of 23 years, was already turning the TV set on, he always watched the news while he ate. Sparky stopped eating when he saw the photographs of the two young men flash on the screen. He jumped up from the table and turned up the volume.

"…These men are considered armed and dangerous, anyone having knowledge of their whereabouts are urged to contact the Department of Public Safety immediately."

The newscaster continued with other local news.

Sparky's face was ashen as he sank into his chair. "What's wrong Spark?" Carolyn asked pretending not to know why he was acting so funny.

At first, he didn't answer his wife then he raised his hand to acknowledge that he had heard her. A minute or so later he said, "Billy has got himself into some real trouble."

"Maybe it wasn't Billy."

Sparky Stillman knew that it was Bill Carey's face that he had just seen on the news broadcast. He also knew what had to be done next. He walked slowly to the door then turned to face Carolyn. Sparky answered his wife's unspoken question. "I have to Carolyn, it's my civic duty."

Sparky Stillman drove directly to the Sherman PD and told them all he knew about his nephew, Bill Carey. Joe and Miller were there when he arrived. After he had finished with his statement Miller said, "Stillman there ain't many people I know that would inform the police about their relatives. What's your motive?" Miller did not have to wait long for Spark's reaction to the suggestive question.

"Motive? I ain't got no damned motive, it's my civic duty to keep these fools off the streets." Stillman displayed his anger.

Miller believed Stillman was truthful now, so he paid more attention to the man's answers. Miller asked, "Do you have any suggestions on where we can find your nephew?"

"If I was looking for him, I'd say head towards Austin. That's where he went to college, and he mentioned something about heading that way." Sparky Stillman felt good, he knew he was doing the right thing, after all it was his civic duty.

Chapter Twenty-Eight
Austin Rescue

A teletype message describing Carey and Lansky preceded Joe and Miller to Austin. By the time they arrived they were exhausted. The human body can only withstand so much abuse. Some of the Austin police had been getting the word onto the streets about the kidnappers, in hopes of getting some kind of lead.

Three days after their arrival, on Wednesday, Joe and his captain made contact with the Austin PD. They received a warm welcome and were assured they would be extended any assistance they required by their colleagues.

The most valuable lead came the next day from a young patrolman, Krinshaw. It seems Krinshaw had been discussing Carey and Lansky with his father, who owned a Gulf station in Austin. Mr. Krinshaw had seen two men watching the description of the kidnappers at his station recently. An attendant at the station had known one of the suspects. Officer Krinshaw had asked his father to find out where the suspects were staying. He had succeeded and the information had been relayed to Joe Ruddy.

The windshield of the Charger suddenly shattered, spraying glass all over the interior of the car. The bullet was stopped by Miller's meaty left shoulder. Joe glanced from the corner of his eye and saw the blood spurting from the wound. Miller, if he was hurting, gave no outward indication of his pain. Just another battle injury.

The information had been correct. Someone was in the house and they did not care for company. The greeting that had just been displayed to Joe and Captain Miller was proof of that. They had no sooner pulled into the driveway when the shooting started. Joe could not stop the vehicle; he and Miller would be sitting ducks if they were to remain in the vehicle or if they attempted to get out of the car. The only choice Joe had was to floor the accelerator and aim the car at the source of the gunfire.

The Charger was transformed into a guided missile as it crashed through the side of the house and through the window. The unfriendly gunman had stood there just seconds before. Joe and Miller were out of the Charger and rolling on the floor of the demolished front room before the car had stopped its forward motion. The two kidnappers were totally surprised and immediately surrendered. They wanted no part of these two crazy gangbusters.

Miller handcuffed one of the men while Joe restrained the other.

"Where's the girl?" Joe demanded.

"She's in the back," answered Joe's prisoner.

Joe went to the back to find Andrea while Miller herded the two men onto a sofa in the corner of the room. Miller then called the Austin PD and requested a car to pick them up. The Charger would require some repairs before it would be operational again.

In a few minutes Joe returned to the front of the house. "She seems to be in pretty good shape. We better get an ambulance out here though, she's gonna need a checkup."

"You go on back and take care of her, I'll call the PD for the ambulance," Miller offered.

About twenty minutes had expired before the first police car arrived. Miller gave the uniformed policemen custody of the two kidnappers and told them he and Joe would be by the station later to book the prisoners. A few minutes later the medical unit arrived. The paramedics examined Andrea and advised Joe that she was in stable condition.

"She has sustained bruises and contusions but her vital signs are strong. But she will require a complete physical before she will be allowed to travel."

"Joe you go ahead and ride in with the ambulance and I'll arrange to get this mess cleaned up." Miller indicated the Charger and the hole in the front of the house.

Joe climbed into the rear of the ambulance with Andrea and the vehicle sped north on the deserted highway. After the excitement had subsided Miller found himself alone in the strange house. His left shoulder began to throb, a sharp pain throughout his arm suddenly made him more aware of the gunshot wound, which was now more than an hour old. Captain Miller called the police department once again and requested a tow truck.

Outside, in the rear of the house, Miller found the VW that Sparky Stillman had described. A search of the car disclosed a sawed-off shotgun. Miller was sure the same shotgun that had been used on his old friend Don Vander.

About an hour later the tow truck arrived. Miller helped the driver make the hook up then asked, "Could you drop me by the hospital?"

"Sure. Say Mister it looks like you caught a slug," said the driver.

"Ah, it's nothing," Miller replied.

In the emergency treatment room at the hospital, Miller was waiting to be patched up when Joe entered the room.

"How bad is it Captain?"

"Just a scratch. Hell, them boys went elephant hunting with a .22." Miller laughed.

By the time Miller arrived at the Austin PD he was peppery. "Where's the son-of-a-bitch that shot me? I'm going to kick the little fucker's ass."

"Hey boss, calm down. We want a conviction on these two. Right now, we have a good case let's not take a chance on losing it on some technicality."

Miller did not appreciate Joe impeding his anger. He had not had a chance to release the pressure that had been building for a long time. He knew Joe was right. If he plunged into the interrogation room and started pounding a prisoner, he could be charged with unnecessary force, if not assault and battery. The case against the two kidnappers would be thrown out of court. It didn't seem like justice, but it was the law.

Captain Miller felt defanged. But his display of anger had relieved him to a degree.

"I'm alright Joe. It's just been awhile. I guess I just forgot how to control my temper." Miller relented.

"Okay Captain. Now let's go in there and question these assholes." Joe was relieved.

The Dallas police officers were not in the interrogation room ten minutes before the tension started to build. Bill Carey was a shit house lawyer and was unwilling to talk. Lansky wanted to confess but he had been instructed by Carey to not say anything. Miller attempted several interrogative techniques, but none were successful. Finally, Miller surrendered and decided that he would rather start again in the morning.

"I'm tired Joe. I guess I lost a little blood. I'm going to get some sleep and try again tomorrow. You staying?"

"I think I will Captain. I'll see you in a while. I'm going to try one more thing on these no talking assholes."

"Bonham General, may I help you?"

"Yes, I'm Captain Miller with the Dallas PD. I'm checking on the condition of Don Vander."

"One moment sir, I'll pull his chart," the night nurse was friendly. Miller knew what had been causing his strange behavior since he had started working on this case. He had been concerned about Don Vander. It could just as easily have been Miller lying in the hospital recovering from a shotgun blast.

"Sir his condition has stabilized. He has been moved from ICU. You can go through the switchboard and connect with his room if you'd like."

Miller jotted the room number. "Thanks." He said. A few minutes later his tension had eased considerably.

"John Miller? Damn it's good to hear from you John!" Vander was pleased with news of the arrests of his assailants. "You located those bastards fast Johnny. Any resistance?"

"No Don. Piece of cake." Miller lied, not wanting to upset the recovering Vander.

After some reminiscing the two old friends said goodnight. Both men were more relaxed, and sleep came instantly.

Joe Ruddy had been piecing together his last technique since he had been assigned to this case. Bits and pieces from all stages of the investigation. With some known facts and some imagination, he could construct a fairly accurate account of the crimes Carey and Lansky had committed. With any luck he would have the two men despising each other before midnight. The next hoped-for result would have the two thugs filling in the shaded areas with confessions.

By midnight Joe was ready to admit his inability to obtain a confession from either man. One last attempt and he would meet the kidnappers/attempted murderers at arraignment court in the morning.

Unexpectedly Lansky started to sing, "I told him we would never get away with it. I had no idea he would go so far as to shoot a cop."

Joe wasted no time in recording the confession. He had Lansky sign the document then left the station at about 1:00 A.M. If Joe Ruddy had ever needed a Jack Daniel's and coke, he needed one now.

The next morning the effect of the drugs had worn off and Andrea Peters was perky. Joe had stopped by the hospital after Carey and Lansky had been arraigned. His role in this investigation should have been complete with the exception of the trial, which would be a few months later. Right, it should have been and would have been if he had not visited Andrea before returning to Dallas.

Yesterday, when he had found her at the house with her captors, she had been heavily sedated. Today she appeared very cautious as she answered Ruddy's routine questions. She was particularly concerned with what she had talked about while she had been under the influence of the sedatives.

"What was I babbling about on the way to the hospital yesterday? I knew I was talking but it was like I was dreaming. I cannot remember who I talked to or what I said. Did I say anything stupid?"

Joe suddenly had a strange thought-So many people had secrets. What dark secret could this beautiful young lady be so frightened of revealing.

The anxiety was there as an embryo at first. A sticky embryo that collected substance as Joe rolled it through his deductive head. When Joe Ruddy had entered the heiress' hospital room moments earlier, she had been nothing more than an attractive victim. Suddenly she had taken on a new role. Andrea Peters was currently starring in a play that Joe was directing in the theater of his thoughts. She had become the subject of an investigation, a Joe Ruddy investigation.

At noon Joe contacted the garage he had hired to do the repair work on his Charger. He was informed that it would be at least another day before the repairs would be completed. Miller decided not to wait. He made connections for a flight returning to Dallas that afternoon.

At 1:00 P.M., somewhat disappointed that he had not had the opportunity to kick ass or to test fire his new .44 magnum, Miller boarded his Dallas flight.

Once again Joe was alone, in Austin, with nothing to do. Jack Daniel's would help him think of something-or help him not to think at all. The latter being what Joe Ruddy preferred at times. But subliminal thoughts of Andrea plagued him. What fate had brought him from Dallas to make the Austin rescue?

Chapter Twenty-Nine
Nashville Calling

Old cases, Joe was methodically reviewing the old cases to determine which one he should investigate next. The last old case he had revived had begun as a simple attempted extortion, if there was such a thing. He had been about to close the case when he had been sucked into kidnapping, not to mention the attempted murder of a police officer. Nothing is ever simple, he thought.

Joe was back in Dallas it had been over a week since the shootout in Austin still he could not shake this feeling he had about Andrea Peters. The whole ordeal had been suspicious. He tossed the case file on the desk, stood and stretched his stiff body.

"Harmon, I'll be on a case. I'll keep my beeper on if you need me, give me a beep."

"You got it," Harmon, the black detective replied.

Joe had to somehow gain access to the closet inside Andrea's mind. Maybe he could stumble over some calcium deposits. He strongly suspected that she was hiding some skeletons there. On the pretense of following up his investigation Joe paid Andrea Peters a visit.

When he arrived at the plantation style mansion Andrea's Jaguar was in the drive. It was the maid's day off, so she was there alone. She was pleased to see the man who had rescued her. "I didn't have a chance to properly thank you for rescuing me. I was pretty shook up at the time." she said.

"Just doing my duty." Joe answered modestly.

As Joe was led into the house, he admired the paintings on the walls. One in particular, a portrait of a lady, held Joe's attention throughout his short visit with Andrea. He could not concentrate fully on Andrea with his mind so fixed on the portrait. As he was about to leave Joe could contain his curiosity no longer, "Who is the lady in the painting?" He asked.

"That's my mother. She's dead now. She was a beautiful woman, don't you agree?"

"Oh, yes ma'am," Joe was awed at the striking resemblance, the lady in the portrait could have been Susan Jordon, a few years earlier. He said goodbye to Andrea and left. Joe headed straight home and to bed, he was exhausted.

Later that evening, while dreaming, he went to see Julie. The Torn Dollar was in full swing at 7:30. Three of the five or so regulars were already at the bar, Julie was there, bored as usual. She had her eyes glued to a gossip magazine and did not see Joe come in. He stood for a few minutes, directly in front of her. When she did not look up from the magazine Joe said, "This place is dead tonight."

"Joe, when did you come in?" she asked, putting the gossip book away.

"I've been here since the article on Michael Jackson," Joe laughed, "I see this place is crowded again tonight," he commented, glancing around the room.

"Barely enough room to squeeze between the tables," Julie replied sarcastically.

By now Julie had placed a Jack Daniel's in front of Joe, he drank it and stood up. "How about another one? Make it a double I'll be right back." He walked outside and returned a few minutes later with his guitar. He placed the instrument on the stage and went back to the bar. "I thought tonight would be a good time to try my music on this crowd. There's not many here so the worst that could happen is they all leave." Joe said. Julie was excited, "They'll love it."

Joe had another Jack Daniel's and headed for the stage. He made some adjustments, hooked up the guitar to the house amplifying system, tested the microphone then he was ready to begin. The Ovation was comforting as he strapped it over his shoulder, but Jack Daniel's was what had calmed his nerves. Joe chorded the guitar and started with a Hank Williams ballad, "...Goodbye Joe me gotta go me oh my oh..."

When the song was finished there was no applause, but Joe was not discouraged. The next song was one of Bob Wills' old songs. No true Texan could sit still for a Bob Wills number, no one except the customers at the Torn Dollar saloon. Julie's was the only applause. In fact, she was the only one in the nightclub who did not display a perfunctory attitude towards Joe's performance.

An impatient man would have admitted defeat but Joe was not an impatient man when it came to music, he continued; "We don't smoke marijuana in Muskogee, we don't take our trips on LSD, we don't burn our draft cards down on main street cause we like living right and being free…" The applause frightened Joe at first. At the end of the song he said, "I see we have some Merle Haggard fans here tonight."

One of the older men stood up and shouted drunkenly, "No boy, we are just all a bunch of Okies and that's our theme song." Joe's indomitable nature would not allow him to submit to the paying customer's discord he wailed a final Hank Williams ballad then returned to the bar.

The old man had been succinct, the public was interested in hearing songs they could relate to. If he was going to ascend in the music business Joe would have to constantly change with the audience. There would always be songs that any audience would accept-the immortal songs, but innovation was the key to success. One true statement uttered by a gray-haired old man had been his inspiration. Joe Ruddy was about to commence a musical venture that would astound the music industry.

The constant ringing of the telephone eventually woke Joe. How long had he been asleep? At least three hours, maybe longer. He picked up the receiver and the long-distance operator's voice said, "Joe Ruddy? Nashville calling."

"It sure is," he said thinking about the dream he had just been awakened from. "It sure is."

Chapter Thirty
So Long

The hot Texas sun was overhead, the August heat miserable. Interstate 35 was spotted with over-heated vehicles pulled alongside the road waiting for their owners to return with water. Joe Ruddy had seen this sight before, mechanical assists in the Dallas heat could become a nightmare for any patrolman.

Today he was not on duty, Joe had taken a week leave of absence and was on his way to Nashville. Susan Jordan had called and practically begged him to come and record an album. Joe had been reluctant at first but here he was in his Charger driving north on I-35. Lately he had been thinking about quitting the police force; the demands were becoming greater but the pay not increasing comparably.

He leaned forward and turned the car stereo on. Merle Haggard's rugged country voice filled the car with, "Let's chase each other round the room tonight..." He's done it again thought Joe. Merle's got another hit. Haggard's number one fan was not surprised Joe had always said Merle could sing the Gettysburg Address and make the top ten with it.

Writing songs had become more than a whim for Joe since he had visited Nashville. He had thought about the recording industry a lot but was not completely convinced that he should dive into the music industry without a lifeline. Like any big profit industry, a novice could find himself in over his head. The right connection was what he needed, and he hoped Susan Jordon was that connection.

Late that same evening Joe entered the Nashville city limits on I-40. He had returned to Music City, USA for the purpose of recording the album but his first stop was the Nashville PD. Ray Cauley was on duty and surprised to see Joe. "Where you staying?" he asked.

"I don't have a place yet. I thought I would see how I stand with Carla."

"She's cold Joe, I guess you don't get the Nashville news in Dallas."

"What the fuck are you talking about Ray?"

"About a week ago Carla was killed in an accident, hit-and-run. Not a trace of a lead." Ray informed the shocked Ruddy.

The two men talked for several minutes then Ray had to leave. Joe had not been prepared for the news of Carla's death. He still could not believe it. Murder? Or an accident? Every time Joe entered this city someone seemed to get murdered, it was a depressing thought.

At noon the next day Joe drove to 612 Magnolia he wanted to get his recording business completed and return to Dallas. He was starting to dislike this city all over again. The Texas license plates on the Jaguar parked in Susan's drive seemed out of place. What was more disturbing the vehicle looked familiar.

Inside the house Susan and Andrea were becoming acquainted. Andrea had known for two years now that Susan was her real mother. She had waited until her inheritance was firmly secure before attempting to contact Susan, she could not take a chance on losing 12 million dollars.

The ladies were interrupted by the sound of the doorbell. Susan answered the door and responded to Joe's presence in her normal way. "Dam Joe Ruddy, it's good to see you!" Joe's eyes rested briefly on the typing desk where Carla had spent so much time. He half expected her to be there typing. He glanced away and allowed Susan to take his hand and lead him into the recording studio.

Several minutes had gone by and when Susan still had not mentioned anything about Carla's death Joe interjected. "So, what's the story on Carla?"

"It was an unfortunate thing Joe. She was struck by a car just a week ago, it killed her instantly."

His enthusiasm had suddenly waned, he no longer cared about anything-not recording-not police work, he had not realized Carla had meant so much to him. He told Susan he would call her later then left.

Seconds later Joe was in his Charger driving to nowhere specific when he remembered that Susan's car had not been in the drive. She had always left her Caddie outside. No, it couldn't be, Joe put the thought of murder aside.

When Susan returned to the kitchen, she found Andrea nearly hysterical. "That was Joe Ruddy out there. He's a Dallas policeman and he may have recognized my car. What did he want with me?"

"Calm down honey, he wasn't looking for you, he was here to do a recording." Susan told Andrea all about her association with Joe Ruddy. Then the reconciled mother and daughter had a long discussion of the years they had not spent together.

Nashville gave Joe the creeps. He stopped for coffee at Denny's and to sort out his priorities. He was not in the mood for anything constructive at the moment, especially since Carla had so recently been killed. After his third cup of coffee he had made a career decision to decline the recording offer. He may regret it later, but he'd had his fill of the murder industry and called Susan to tell her so.

"If you're sure that's what you want Joe, then goodbye," Susan choked the words.

"I'll just say so long. Remember Susan, Carla's death has not been solved so I could drop in again sometime. Good luck in the murder industry."

Andrea Peters had no reason to fear anyone legally taking her inheritance. She believed otherwise, since she had learned that Susan was her true mother, she had feared that James Peters had not really been her father, but she would never reveal her thoughts to anyone. Susan would not discuss Andrea's father, avoiding all questions concerning him. She would neither confirm nor deny that Peters was the legitimate father. It was one of Susan's secrets that she would not reveal to anyone.

The father of Susan Moore's discarded baby girl was none other than James Peters, and they had been married, however brief. Five years ago, she had unexpectedly met James while she had been in Dallas. After all those years she still hated the man for deserting her and the baby girl. Susan was no longer the naive young girl from Toledo.

Right after her visit to Dallas, Susan had a strange discussion with a doctor friend, concerning nontraceable death producing drugs. She had been especially interested in the ones that produced the exact same symptoms of cardiac arrest.

Susan Jordon hugged her newly reunited offspring and thought, it's a long way from Toledo to the music, or-what had Joe Ruddy called it? - The Murder Industry.

THE END

About the Author

A.R. Ratliff was born on June 11, 1951 in Beattyville, KY. He served in the U.S. Army for seven years as an MP around Bamberg, Germany. He continued his service in the U.S. Navy for 14 years and retired at the rank of Chief Master at Arms with an honorable discharge in 1994. He wrote the story of Detective Joe Ruddy while serving in the Navy, utilizing his knowledge of law enforcement and his love for mystery. He received many medals of commendation throughout his military career including a Navy Achievement Medal, a National Defense Service Medal, Rifle Marksman ribbons, and an expert pistol shot medal.

Throughout his life, A.R. charmed many with his musical talents and his quick wit. He was a musician since childhood, playing country guitar, writing, and singing hundreds of original songs. Sadly, A.R. passed away in 2011 after a bout with cancer. This book was a labor of love for him and is being published as a tribute to him and for his years of service as well as the years of love and joy that he provided for family and friends all over the world. He will forever be missed by those who knew and loved him.

Other titles from Higher Ground Books & Media:

In the Wash: The Rona Shively Stories by Rebecca Benston

(And the entire Rona Shively Stories series)

Jack Kramer's Journey by Frank Adkins

Wise Up to Rise Up by Rebecca Benston

A Path to Shalom by Steen Burke

Dear You by Derra Nicole Sabo

I Don't Want to Be Like You by Maryanne Christiano-Mistretta

Miracles: I Love Them by Forest Godin

Out of Darkness by Stephen Bowman

Shameless Persistence by Sandra Bretting

My Name is Sam by Joe Siccardi

Chronicles of a Spiritual Journey by Stephen Shepherd

Add these titles to your collection today!

http://highergroundbooksandmedia.com

Do you have a story to tell?

Higher Ground Books & Media is an independent Christian-based publisher specializing in stories of triumph! Our purpose is to empower, inspire, and educate through the sharing of personal experiences.

Please visit our website for our submission guidelines.

http://www.highergroundbooksandmedia.com

www.ingramcontent.com/pod-product-compliance
Lightning Source LLC
Chambersburg PA
CBHW031337170626
46807CB00002B/749